TRISTESSA

TRISTESSA

Jack Kerouac

McGraw-Hill Book Company

New York St. Louis San Francisco Bogotá Düsseldorf
Madrid Mexico Montreal Panama Paris
São Paulo Tokyo Toronto

First McGraw-Hill Paperback edition, 1978

  5 6 7 8 9 10 11   BKP BKP   8 9 8 7

ISBN 0-07-034205-9

PART ONE

Trembling and Chaste

I'M RIDING ALONG with Tristessa in the cab, drunk, with big bottle of Juarez Bourbon whiskey in the till-bag railroad lootbag they'd accused me of holding in railroad 1952—here I am in Mexico City, rainy Saturday night, mysteries, old dream sidestreets with no names reeling in, the little street where I'd walked through crowds of gloomy Hobo Indians wrapped in tragic shawls enough to make you cry and you thought you saw knives flashing beneath the folds—lugubrious dreams as tragic as the one of Old Railroad Night where my father sits big of thighs in smoking car of night, outside's a brakeman with red light and white light, lumbering in the sad vast mist tracks of life—but now I'm up on that Vegetable plateau Mexico, the moon of Citlapol a few nights earlier I'd stumbled to on the sleepy roof on the way to the ancient dripping stone toilet—Tristessa is high, beautiful as ever, goin home gayly to go to bed and enjoy her morphine.

Night before I've in a quiet hassel in the rain sat with her darkly at Midnight counters eating bread and soup and drinking Delaware Punch, and I'd come out of that interview with a vision of Tristessa in my bed in my arms, the strangeness of her love-cheek, Azteca, Indian girl with mysterious lidded Billy Holliday eyes and spoke with great melancholic voice like Luise Rainer sadfaced Viennese actresses that made all Ukraine cry in 1910.

Gorgeous ripples of pear shape her skin to her cheekbones, and long sad eyelids, and Virgin Mary resignation, and peachy coffee complexion and eyes of astonishing mystery with nothing-but-earth-depth expressionless half disdain and half mournful lamentation of pain. "I am seek," she's always saying to me and Bull at the pad—I'm in Mexico City wildhaired and mad riding in a cab down past the Ciné Mexico in rainy traffic jams, I'm swigging from the bottle, Tristessa is trying long harangues to explain that the night before when I put her in the cab the driver'd tried to make her and she hit him with her fist, news which the present driver receives without comment—We're going down to Tristessa's house to sit and get high—Tristessa has warned me that the house will be a mess because her sister is drunk and sick, and El Indio will be there standing majestically with morphine needle downward in the big brown arm, glitter-eyed looking right at you or expecting the prick of the needle to bring the wanted flame itself and going "Hm-za . . . the Aztec needle in my flesh of flame" looking all a whole lot like the big cat in Culiao who presented me the 0 the time I came down to Mexico to see other visions—My whiskey bottle has strange Mexican soft covercap that I keep worrying will slip off and all my bag be drowned in Bourbon 86 proof whiskey.

Through the crazy Saturday night drizzle streets like Hong Kong our cab pushes slowly through the Market ways and we come out on the whore street district and get off behind the fruity fruitstands and tortilla beans and tacos shacks with fixed wood benches—It's the poor district of Rome.

I pay the cab 3.33 by giving cabbie 10 pesos and asking "seis" for change, which I get without comment and wonder if Tristessa thinks I am too splurgy like big John Drunk in Mexico—But no time to think, we are hurrying through the slicky sidewalks of glisten-neon reflections and candle lights of little sidewalk sitters with walnuts on a towel for sale—turn quickly at the stinky alleyway of her tenement cell-house one story high—We go through dripping faucets and pails and boys and duck under wash and come to her iron door, which from adobe withins is unlocked and we step in the kitchen the rain still falling from the leaves and boards that served as the kitchen roof—allowing little drizzles to fizzle in the kitchen over the chicken garbage in the damp corner—Where, miraculously, now, I see the little pink cat taking a little pee on piles of okra and chickenfeed—The inside bedroom is littered completely and ransacked as by madmen with torn newspapers and the chicken's pecking at the rice and the bits of sandwiches on the floor—On the bed lay Tristessa's "sister" sick, wrapped in pink coverlet—it's as tragic as the night Eddy was shot on the rainy Russia Street—

TRISTESSA IS SITTING on the edge of the bed adjusting her nylon stockings, she pulls them awkwardly from her shoes with big sad face overlooking her endeavors with pursy lips, I watch the way she twists her feet inward convulsively when she looks at her shoes.

  She is such a beautiful girl, I wonder what all my friends would say back in New York and up in San Francisco, and what would happen down in Nola when you see her cutting down Canal Street in the hot sun and she has dark glasses and a lazy walk and keeps trying to tie her kimono to her thin overcoat as though the kimono was supposed to tie to the coat, tugging convulsively at it and goofing in the street saying "Here ees the cab—hey hees hey who—there you go—I breeng you back the m o a - n y." Money's moany. She makes money sound like my old French Canadian Aunt in Lawrence "It's not you moany, that I want, it's you l o a v e"—Love is loave. "Eets you l a w v." The law is lawv.—Same with Tristessa, she is so high all the time, and sick, shooting ten gramos of morphine per month,—staggering down the city streets yet so beautiful people keep turning and looking at her—Her eyes are radiant and shining and her cheek is wet from the mist and her Indian hair is

black and cool and slick hangin in 2 pigtails behind with
the roll-sod hairdo behind (the correct Cathedral Indian
hairdo)—Her shoes she keeps looking at are brand new
not scrawny, but she lets her nylons keep falling and
keeps pulling on them and convulsively twisting her
feet—You picture what a beautiful girl in New York,
wearing a flowery wide skirt a la New Look with Dior
flat bosomed pink cashmere sweater, and her lips and
eyes do the same and do the rest. Here she is reduced
to impoverished Indian Lady gloomclothes—You see the
Indian ladies in the inscrutable dark of doorways, looking like holes in the wall not women—their clothes—and
you look again and see the brave, the noble *mujer*, the
mother, the woman, the Virgin Mary of Mexico.—Tristessa has a huge ikon in a corner of her bedroom.

It faces the room, back to the kitchen wall, in right
hand corner as you face the woesome kitchen with its
drizzle showering ineffably from the roof tree twigs and
hammberboards (bombed out shelter roof)—Her ikon
represents the Holy Mother staring out of her blue char-
aderees, her robes and Damema arrangements, at which
El Indio prays devoutly when going out to get some
junk. El Indio is a vendor of curios, allegedly,—I never
see him on San Juan Letran selling crucifixes, I never
see El Indio in the street, no Redondas, no anywhere—
The Virgin Mary has a candle, a bunch of glass-fulla-
wax economical burners that go for weeks on end, like
Tibetan prayer-wheels the inexhaustible aid from our
Amida—I smile to see this lovely ikon—

Around it are pictures of the dead—When Tristessa wants to say "dead" she clasps her hands in holy attitude, indicating her Aztecan belief in the holiness of death, by same token the holiness of the essence—So she has photo of dead Dave my old buddy of previous years now dead of high blood pressure at age 55—His vague Greek-Indian face looks out from pale indefinable photograph. I can't see him in all that snow. He's in heaven for sure, hands V-clasped in eternity ecstasy of Nirvana. That's why Tristessa keeps clasping her hands and praying, saying, too, "I love Dave," she had loved her former master—He had been an old man in love with a young girl. At 16 she was an addict. He took her off the street and, himself an addict of the street, redoubled his energies, finally made contact with wealthy junkies and showed her how to live—once a year together they'd taken hikes to Chalmas to the mountain to climb part of it on their knees to come to the shrine of piled crutches left there by pilgrims healed of disease, the thousand *tapete*-straws laid out in the mist where they sleep the night out in blankets and raincoats—returning, devout, hungry, healthy, to light new candles to the Mother and hitting the street again for their morphine—God knows where they got it.

I sit admiring that majestical mother of lovers.

THERE'S NO DESCRIBING the awfulness of that gloom in the holes in the ceiling, the brown halo of the

night city lost in a green vegetable height above the
Wheels of the Blakean adobe rooftops—Rain is blearing
now on the green endlessness of the Valley Plain north
of Actopan—pretty girls are dashing over gutters full
of pools—Dogs bark at hirshing cars—The drizzle emp-
ties eerily into the kitchen's stone Dank, and the door
glistens (iron) all shiney and wet—The dog is howling
in pain on the bed.—The dog is the little Chihuahua
mother 12 inches long, with fine little feet with black
toes and toenails, such a "fine" and delicate dog you
couldnt touch her without she'd squeal in pain—
"Y- e e e - p" All you could do was snap your finger gently
at her and allow her to nip-nose her cold little wet snout
(black as a bull's) against your fingernails and thumb.
Sweet little dog—Tristessa says she's in heat and that's
why she cries—The rooster screams beneath the bed.

All this time the rooster's been listening under the
springs, meditating, turning to look all around in his
quiet darkness, the noise of the golden humans above
" B e u - v e u - V A A?" he screams, he howls, he inter-
rupts a half a dozen simultaneous conversations raging
like torn paper above—The hen chuckles.

The hen is outside, wandering among our feet, pecking gently at the floor—She digs the people. She wants
to come up near me and rub illimitably against my pant
leg, but I dont give her encouragement, in fact havent
noticed her yet and it's like the dream of the vast mad
father of the wild barn in howling Nova Scotia with the
floodwaters of the sea about to engulf the town and
surrounding pine countrysides in the endless north—It

was Tristessa, Cruz on the bed, El Indio, the cock, the dove on the mantelpiece top (never a sound except occasional wing flap practice), the cat, the hen, and the bloody howling woman dog blacky Espana Chihuahua pooch bitch.

El Indio's eyedropper is completely full, he jabs in the needle hard and it's dull and it wont penetrate the skin and he jabs in harder and works it in but instead of wincing waits open mouthed with ecstasy and gets the dropful in, down, standing,—"You've got to do me a favor Mr. Gazookus," says Old Bull Gaines interrupting my thought, "come down to Tristessa's with me—I've run short—" but I'm bursting to explode out of sight of Mexico City with walking in the rain splashing through puddles not cursing nor interested but just trying to get home to bed, dead.

It's the raving bloody book of dreams of the cursing world, full of suits, dishonesties and written agreements. And briberies, to children for their sweets, to children for their sweets. "Morphine is for pain," I keep thinking, "and the rest is rest. It is what it is, I am what I am, Adoration to Tathagata, Sugata, Buddha, perfect in Wisdom and Compassion who has accomplished, and is accomplishing, and will accomplish, all these words of mystery."

—Reason I bring the whiskey, to drink, to crash through the black curtain—At same time a comedian in the city in the night—Bepestered by glooms and lull intervenes, bored, drinking, curtsying, crashing, "Where

I'm gonna do,"—I pull the chair up to the corner of the foot of the bed so I can sit between the kitty and the Virgin Mary. The kitty, *la gata* in Spanish, the little Tathagata of the night, golden pink colored, 3 weeks old, crazy pink nose, crazy face, eyes of green, mustachio'd golden lion forceps and whiskers—I run my finger over her little skull and she pops up purring and the little purring-machine is started for awhile and she looks around the room glad watching what we're all doing.— "She's having golden thoughts," I'm thinking.—Tristessa likes eggs otherwise she wouldnt allow a male rooster in this female establishment? How should I know how eggs are made. On my right the devotional candles flame before the clay wall.

IT'S INFINITELY WORSE than the sleeping dream I've had of Mexico City where I go dreary along empty white apartments, gray, alone, or where the marble steps of a hotel horrify me—It's the rainy night in Mexico City and I'm in the middle of Mexico Thieves Market district and El Indio is a wellknown thief and even Tristessa was a pickpocket but I dont do more than flick my backhand against the bulge of my folded money sailorwise stowed in the railroad watchpocket of my jeans—And in shirtpocket I have the travelers checks which are unstealable in a sense—That, Ah that side street where the gang of Mexicans stop me and rifle through my dufflebag and

take what they want and take me along for a drink—It's
gloom as unpredicted on this earth, I realize all the
uncountable manifestations the thinking-mind invents
to place wall of horror before its pure perfect realization
that there is no wall and no horror just Transcendental
Empty Kissable Milk Light of Everlasting Eternity's true
and perfectly empty nature.—I know everything's alright but I want proof and the Buddhas and the Virgin
Marys are there reminding me of the solemn pledge of
faith in this harsh and stupid earth where we rage our
so-called lives in a sea of worry, meat for Chicagos of
Graves—right this minute my very father and my very
brother lie side by side in mud in the North and I'm
supposed to be smarter than they are—being quick I am
dead. I look up at the others glooping, they see I've been
lost in thought in my corner chair but are pursuing
endless wild worries (all mental 100%) of their own—
They're yakking in Spanish, I only understand snatches
of that virile conversation—Tristessa keeps saying
"chinga" at every other sentence, a swearing Marine,—
she says it with scorn and her teeth bite and it makes
me worry 'Do you know women as well as you think you
do?'—The rooster is unperturbed and lets go a blast.

I TAKE OUT my whiskey bottle from the bag, the Canady
Dry, open both, and pour me a hiball in a cup—making
one too for Cruz who has just jumped outa bed to throw

up on the kitchen floor and now wants another drink, she's been in the cantina for women all day somewhere back near the whore district of Panama Street and sinister Rayon Street with its dead dog in the gutter and beggars on the sidewalk with no hats looking at you helplessly—Cruz is a little Indian woman with no chin and bright eyes and wears high heel pumps without stockings and battered dresses, what a wild crew of people, in America a cop would have to do a double take seeing them pass all be-wrongled and arguing and staggering on the sidewalk, like apparitions of poverty— Cruz takes a hiball and throws it up too. Nobody notices, El Indio is holding eyedropper in one hand and little piece of paper in the other arguing, tense necked, red, fullblast at a screaming Tristessa whose bright eyes dance to fight it out—The old lady Cruz groans from the riot of it and buries back in her bed, the only bed, under her blanket, her face bandaged and greasy, the little black dog curling against her, and the cat, and she is lamenting something, her drink sickness, and El Indio's constant harassing for more of Tristessa's supply of morphine—I gulp my drink.

Next door the mother's made the little daughter cry, we can hear her praying little woeful squeals enough to make a father's heart break and maybe it might be,— Trucks pass, buses, loud, growling, loaded to the springs with people riding to Tacuyaba and Rastro and Circumvalacion round-routeries of town—the streets of mess puddles that I am going to walk home in at 2 A M

splashing without care through streetpools, looking
along lone fences at the dismal glimmer of the wet rain
shinning in the streetlight—The pit and horror of my
grit, the Virya tense-neck muscles that a man needs to
steel his teeth together to press through lonely roads of
rain at night with no hope of a warm bed—My head
fells and wearies to think of it. Tristessa says "How is
Jack,—?—" She always asks: "Why are you so sad??—
'Muy dolorosa' " and as though to mean "You are very
full of pain," for pain means *dolor*—"I am sad because
all la vida es dolorosa," I keep replying, hoping to teach
her Number One of the Four Great Truths,—Besides,
what could be truer? With her heavy purple eyes she
lids at me the nodding reprisal, 'h a - hum,' Indian-wise
understanding the tone of what I said, and nodding over
it, making me suspicious of the bridge of her nose where
it looks evil and conniving and I think of her as a Houri
Hari Salesman in the hellbottoms Kshitigarbha never
dreamed to redeem.—When she looks like an evil Indian
Joe of Huckleberry Finn, plotting my demise—El Indio,
standing, watching through sad blackened-blue eye
flesh, hard and sharp and clear the side of his face,
darkly hearing that I say All Life is Sad, nods, agreeing,
no comment to make to me or to anyone about it.

Tristessa is bending over the spoon boiling morphine
in it with a match boilerfactory. She looks awkward and
lean and you see the lean hocks of her rear, in the ki-
mono-like crazydress, as she kneels prayer fashion over
the bed boiling her bang over the chair which is cluttered

with ashes, hairpins, cottons, Konk material like strange
Mexican eyelash lippmakers and teasies and greases—
one jiblet of a whole bone of junk, that, had it been
knocked down would have added to the mess on the
floor only a minor further amount of confusion.—"I
raced to find that Tarzan," I'm thinking, remembering
boyhood and home as they lament in the Mexican Saturday Night Bedroom, "but the bushes and the rocks
weren't real and the beauty of things must be that they
end."

I WAIL ON my cup of hiball so much they see I'm going
to get drunk so they all permit me and beseech me to
take a shot of morphine which I accept without fear
because I am drunk—Worse sensation in the world,
to take morphine when you're drunk, the result knots
in your forehead like a rock and makes great pain there
warring in that one field for dominion and none to be
had because they've cancelled out each other the alcohol
and the alkaloid. But I accept, and as soon as I begin
to feel its warning effect and warm effect I look down
and perceive that the chicken, the hen, wants to make
friends with me—She's walking up close with bobbing
neck, looking at my knee cap, looking at my hanging
hands, wants to come close but has no authority—So I
stick my hand out to its beak to be pecked, to let her
know I'm not afraid because I trust her not to hurt me

really—which she doesn't—just stares at my hand rea-
sonably and doubtfully and suddenly almost tenderly
and I pull away my hand with a sense of the victory. She
contentedly chuckles, plucks up a piece of something
from the floor, throws it away, a piece of linen thread
hangs in her beak, she tosses it away, looks around, walks
around the golden kitchen of Time in huge Nirvana
glare of Saturday night and all the rivers roaring in the
rain, the crash inside my soul when I think of babyhood
and you watch the big adults in the room, the wave and
gnash of their shadowy hands, as they harangue about
time and responsibility, in a Golden Movie inside my
own mind without substance not even gelatinous—the
hope and horror of the void—great phantoms screech-
ing inside mind with the yawk photograph VLORK of
the Rooster as he now ups and emits from his throat
intended for open fences of Missouri explodes gunpow-
der blurts of morningshame, reverend for man—At
dawn in impenetrable bleak Oceanities of Undersunk
gloom, he blows his rosy morn Collario and still the
farmer knows it wont tend that rosy way. Then he chuckles, rooster chuckles, comments on something crazy we
might have said, and chuckles—poor sentient noticing
being, the beast he knows his time is up in the Chick-
enshacks of Lenox Avenue—chuckles like we do—yells
louder if a man, with special rooster jowls and jinglets—
Hen, his wife, she wears her adjustible hat falling from
one side of her pretty beak to the other. "Good *morn* ing
Mrs. Gazookas," I tell her, having fun by myself watching

the chickens as I'd done as a boy in New Hampshire in farmhouses at night waiting for the talk to be done and the wood to be taken in. Worked hard for my father in the Pure Land, was strong and true, went to the city to see Tathagata, leveled the ground for his feet, saw bumps everywhere and leveled the ground, he passed by and saw me and said "First level your own mind, and then the earth will be level, even unto Mount Sumeru" (the ancient name for Everest in Old Magadha) (India).

I WANTA MAKE friends with the rooster too, by now I'm sitting in front of the bed in the other chair as El Indio has just gone out with a bunch of suspicious men with mustaches one of whom stared at me curiously and with pleased proud grin as I stood with cup in hand acting drunk before the ladies for his and his friends' edification—Alone in the house with the two women I sit politely before them and we talk earnestly and eagerly about God. "My friends ees seek, I geev them shot," beautiful Tristessa of Dolours is telling me with her long damp expressive fingers dancing little India-Tinkle dances before my haunted eyes."—Eees when, *cuando*, my friend does not pays me back, don I dont care. Because" pointing up with a straight expression into my eyes, finger aloft, "my Lord pay me—and he pay me *more* —M-o-r-e"—she leans quickly emphasizing more, and I wish I could tell her in Spanish the illimitable and

inestimable blessing she will get anyway in Nirvana. But
I love her, I fall in love with her. She strokes my arm
with thin finger. I love it. I'm trying to remember my
place and my position in eternity. I have sworn off lust
with women,—sworn off lust for lust's sake,—sworn off
sexuality and the inhibiting impulse—I want to enter the
Holy Stream and be safe on my way to the other shore,
but would as lief leave a kiss to Tristessa for her hark
of my heart's sake. She knows I admire and love her
with all my heart and that I'm holding myself back. "You
have you life," she says to Old Bull (of whom in a minute)
"and I haff *mind*, mine, and Jack has hees life" indicating
me, she is giving me my life back and not claiming it for
herself as so many of the women you love do claim.—
I love her but I want to leave. She says: "I know it, a
man and women iss dead,—" "when they want to be
dead"—She nods, confirms within herself some dark
Aztecan instinctual belief, wise—a wise woman, who
would have graced the herds of Bhikshunis in very Ya-
sodhara's time and made a divine additional nun. With
her lidded eyes and clasped hands, a Madonna. It makes
me cry to realize Tristessa has never had a child and
probably never will because of her morphine sickness
(a sickness that goes on as long as the need and feeds
off the need and fills in the need simultaneously, so that
she moans from pain all day and the pain is real, like
abcesses in the shoulder and neuralgia down the side of
the head and in 1952 just before Christmas she was
supposed to be dying), holy Tristessa will not be cause

of further rebirth and will go straight to her God and
He will recompense her multibillionfold in aeons and
aeons of dead Karma time. She understands Karma, she
says: "What I do, I *reap*" she says in Spanish—"Men and
women have *errores*—errors, faults, sins, *faltas*," hu-
manbeings sow their own ground of trouble and stumble
over the rocks of their own false erroring imagination,
and life is hard. She knows, I know, you know.—"Bot—
I weeling to haff jonk—morfina—and be no-seek any
more." And she hunches her elbows with peasant face,
understanding herself in a way that I cannot and as I
gaze at her the candlelight flickers on the high cheekbones of her face and she looks as beautiful as Ava
Gardner and even better like a Black Ava Gardner, A
Brown Ava with long face and long bones and long
lowered lids—Only Tristessa hasnt got that expression
of sex-smile, it has the expression of mawkfaced down-
mouthed Indian disregard for what you think about its
own pluperfect beauty. Not that it's perfect beauty like
Ava, it's got faults, errors, but all men and women have
them and so all women forgive men and men forgive
women and go their own holy ways to death. Tristessa
loves death, she goes to the ikon and adjusts flowers and
prays,—She bends over a sandwich and prays, looking
sideways at the ikon, sitting Burmese fashion in the bed
(knee in front of knee) (down) (sitting), she makes a long
prayer to Mary to ask blessing or thanks for the food,
I wait in respectful silence, take a quick peek at El Indio,
who is also devout and even on the point of crying from

junk his eyes moist and reverent and sometimes like especially when Tristessa removes her stockings to get in the bed-blankets an undercurrent of reverent love sayings under his breath ("Tristessa, O Yé, comme t'est Belle") (which is certainly what I'm thinking but afraid to look and watch Tristessa remove her nylons for fear I will get a flash sight of her creamy coffee thighs and go mad)—But El Indio is too loaded with the poison solution of morphine to really care and follow up his reverence for Tristessa, he is busy, sometimes busy being sick, has a wife, two children (down the other side of town), has to work, has to cajole stuff off Tristessa when he himself is out (as now)—(reason for his presence in the house)—I see the whole thing popping and parenthesizing in every direction, the story of that house and that kitchen.

In the kitchen is hanging pictures of Mexican Pornography Girls, with black lace and big thighs and revealing clouds of bosom and pelvic drapery, that I study intently, in the right places, but the pictures (2) are all roiled and rain-stained and roll-spanned and hanging protruding from the wall so you have to straighten them down to study, and even then the rain is misting down through the cabbage leaves above and the soggy cardboard—Who might have tried to make a roof for Fellaheena?—"My Lord, he pay me back *more*"—

SO NOW EL INDIO is back and standing at the head of the bed as I sit there, and I turn to look at the rooster ("to tame him")—I put my hand out exactly as I had done for the hen and allow it to see I'm not scared if it pecks me, and I will pat it and make it free from fear of me—The Rooster gazes at my hand without comment, and looks away, and looks back, and gazes at my hand (the seminal gysmal champion who dreams a daily egg for Tristessa that she sucks out the end after a little puncture, fresh)—he looks at my hand tenderly but majestically moreover as the hen can't make that same majestical appraisal, he's crowned and cocky and can howl, he is the King Fencer biting the duel with that mosey morn. He chuckles at sight of my hand, meaning Yeh and turns away—and I look proudly around to see if Tristessa and El Indio heard my wild *estupiante*—They rave to notice me with avid lips, "Yes we been talkin about the ten gram-mos we gonna get tomorrar—Yeh—" and I feel proud to've made the Rooster, now all the little animals in the room know me and love me and I love them though may not know them. All except The Crooner on the roof, on the clothes closet, in the corner away from the edge, against the wall just under the ceiling, cozy cooing Dove is sitting in nest, ever contemplating the entire scene forever without comment. I look up, my Lord is flapping his wings and coo doving white

and I look at Tristessa to know why she got a dove and
Tristessa lifts up her tender hands helplessly and looks
at me affectionately and sadly, to indicate, "It is my
Pigeon"—"my pretty white Pigeon—what can I do about
it?" "I love it so"—"It is so sweet and white"—"It never
make a noise"—"It got soch prurty eyes you look you
see the prurty eyes" and I look into the eyes of the dove
and they are dove's eyes, lidded, perfect, dark, pools,
mysterious, almost Oriental, unbearable to withstand the
surge of such purity out of eyes—Yet so much like Tristessa's eyes that I wish I could comment and tell Tristessa
'Thou hast the dove's eyes'—

Or every now and then the Dove rises and flaps her
wings for exercise, instead of flying through the bleak
air she waits in her golden corner of the world waiting
for perfect purity of death, the Dove in the grave is a
dark thing to rave—the raven in the grave is no white
light illuminating the Worlds pointing up and pointing
down throughout uppity ten sides of Eternity—Poor
Dove, poor eyes,—her breast white snow, her milk, her
rain of pity over me, her even gentle eye-gaze into mine
from rosy heights on a position in a rack and Arcabus
in the Ope Heavens of the Mind World,—rosy golden
angel of my days, and I can't touch her, wouldn't dare
get up on a chair and trap her in her corner and make
her leery human teeth-grins trying to impress it to my
bloodstained heart—her blood.

EL INDIO HAS brought sandwiches back and the little cat is going crazy for some meat and El Indio gets mad and slaps it off the bed and I throw both hands up at him "Non" "Don't do that" and he doesn't even hear me as Tristessa yells at him—the great Man Beast raging in the kitchen meat and slapping his daughter in her chair clear across the room to tumble on the floor her tears start starting as she realizes what he's done—I don't like El Indio for hitting the cat. But he isn't vicious about it, just merely reprimandatory, stern, justified, dealing with the cat, kicking the cat out of his way in the parlor as he walks to his cigars and Television—Old Father Time is El Indio, with the kids, the wife, the evenings at the supper table slapping the kids away and yornching on great meaty dinners in the dim light—"Blurp, blap," he lets go before the kids who look at him with shining and admiring eyes. Now it's Saturday night and he's dealing with Tristessa and wrangling to explain her, suddenly the old Cruz (who is not old, just 40) jumps up crying "Yeh, with our money, Si, con nuestra dinero" and repeating twice and sobbing and El Indio warns her I might understand (as I look up with imperial magnificence of unconcern tinged by regard for the scene) and as if to say "This woman is crying because you take all their money,—what is this? Russia? Mussia? Matamorapussia? as if I didn't care anyway which I couldnt. All

I wanted to do was get away. I had completely forgotten about the dove and only remembered it days later.

THE WILD WAY Tristessa stands legs spread in the middle of the room to explain something, like a junkey on a corner in Harlem or anyplace, Cairo, Bang Bombayo and the whole Fellah Ollah Lot from Tip of Bermudy to wings of albatross ledge befeathering the Arctic Coastline, only the poison they serve out of Eskimo Gloogloo seals and eagles of Greenland, ain't as bad as that German Civilization morphine she (an Indian) is forced to subdue and die to, in her native earth.

MEANWHILE THE CAT is comfortably ensconced at Cruz's face place where she lies at the foot of the bed, curled, the way she sleeps all night while Tristessa curls at the head and they hook feet like sisters or like mother and daughter and make one little bed do comfortably for two—The little pink kitkat is so certain (despite all his fleas crossing the bridge of his nose or wandering over his eyelids)—that everything is alright—that all is well in the world (at least now)—he wants to be near Cruz's face, where all is well—He (it's a little She) he doesnt notice the bandages and the sorrow and the drunksick horrors she's having, he just knows she's the lady all day her legs are in the kitchen and every now and then she dumps him food, and besides she plays with him on the bed and pretends she's gonna beat him up and holds and scolds him and he yurks in little face into little head and blinks his eyes and flaps back his ears to wait for the beating but she's only playing with him— So now he sits in front of Cruz and even though we may gesture like maniacs as we talk and occasionally a rough hand is waved right by its whiskers almost hitting it or El Indio might roughly decide to throw a newspaper on the bed and land it right on his head, still he sits digging all of us with eyes closed and curled up under Cat Buddha style, meditating among our mad endeavors like the Dove above—I wonder: "Does kittykat know there's a pigeon on the clothes closet." I wish my relatives from Lowell were here to see how people and animals live in Mexico—

But the poor little cat is one mass of fleas, but he doesnt mind, he doesnt keep scratching like American cats but just endures—I pick him up and he's just a skinny little skeleton with great balloons of fur—Everything is so poor in Mexico, people are poor, and yet everything they do is happy and carefree, no matter what is—Tristessa is a junkey and she goes about it skinny and carefree, where an American would be gloomy— But she coughs and complains all day, and by same law, at intervals, the cat explodes into furious scratching that doesnt help—

MEANWHILE I KEEP smoking, my cigarette goes out, and I reach into the ikon for a light from the candle flame, in a glass—I hear Tristessa say something that I interpret to mean "Ack, that stupid fool is using our altar for a light"—To me it's nothing unusual or strange, I just want a light—but perceiving the remark or maintaining belief in the remark without knowing what it was, I ulp and hold back and instead get a light from El Indio, who then shows me later, by quick devout prayer-ito with a piece of newspaper, getting his light indirectly and with a touch and a prayer—Perceiving the ritual I do it too, to get my light a few minutes later—I make a little French prayer: *"Excuse mué ma 'Dame"*—making emphasis on *Dame* because of Damema the Mother of Buddhas.

So I feel less guilty about my smoke and I know all of a sudden all of us will go to heaven straight up from where we are, like golden phantoms of Angels in Gold Strap we go hitch hiking the Deus Ex Machina to heights Apocalyptic, Eucalyptic, Aristophaneac and Divine—I suppose, and I wonder what the cat might think—To Cruz I say "Your cat is having golden thoughts (su gata tienes pensas de or)" but she doesnt understand for a thousand and one billion manifold reasons swimming in the swarm of her milk thoughts Buddha-buried in the stress of her illness enduring—*"What's pensas?"* she

yells to the others, she doesnt know that the cat is having
golden thoughts—But the cat loves her so, and stays
there, little behind to her chin, purring, glad, eyes X-
closed and stoopy, kitty kitkat like the Pinky I'd just lost
in New York run over on Atlantic Avenue by the swerve
dim madtraffics of Brooklyn and Queens, the automa-
tons sitting at wheels automatically killing cats every day
about five or six a day on the same road. "But this cat
will die the normal Mexican death—by old age or disease—and be a wise old big burn in the alleys around,
and you'll see him (dirty as rags) flitting by the garbage
heap like a rat, if Cruz ever gets to throw it out—But
Cruz won't, and so cat stays at her chin-point like a little
sign of her good intentions."

EL INDIO GOES out and gets meat sandwiches and
now the cat goes mad yelling and mewing for some and
El Indio throws her off the bed—but Cat finally gets a
bite of meat and ronches at it like a mad little Tiger and
I think "If she was as big as the one in the Zoo, she'd
look at me with big green eyes before eating me." I'm
having the fairy tale of Saturday night, having a good
time actually because of the booze and the good cheer
and the careless people—enjoying the little animals—
noticing the little Chihuahua pup now meekly waiting
for a bite of meat or bread with her tail curled in and
woe, if she ever inherits the earth it'll be because of

meek—Ears curled back and even whimpering the little
Chihuahua smalldog fear-cry—Nevertheless she's been
alternately watching us and sleeping all night, and her
own reflections on the subject of Nirvana and death and
mortals biding time till death, are of a whimpering high
frequency terrified tender variety—and the kind that
says 'Leave me alone, I am so delicate' and you leave her
alone in her little fragile shell like the shell of canoes
over the ocean deeps—I wish I could communicate to
all these creatures and people, in the flush of my moonshine goodtimes, the cloudy mystery of the magic milk
to be seen in Mind's Deep Imagery where we learn that
everything is nothing—in which case they wouldnt worry
any more, except after the instant they think to worry
again—All of us trembling in our mortality boots, born
to die, BORN TO DIE I could write it on the wall and
on Walls all over America—Dove in wings of peace, with
her Noah Menagery Moonshine eyes; dog with clitty
claws black and shiny, to die is born, trembles in her
purple eyes, her little weak bloodvessels down the ribs;
yea the ribs of Chihuahua, and Tristessa's ribs too, beautiful ribs, her with her aunts in Chihuahua also born to
die, beautiful to be ugly, quick to be dead, glad to be
sad, mad to be had—and the El Indio death, born to
die, the man, so he plies the needle of Saturday Night
every night is Saturday night and goes wild to wait, what
else can he do,—The death of Cruz, the drizzles of re-
ligion falling on her burial fields, the grim mouth planted
the satin of the earth coffin, . . . I moan to recover

all that magic, remembering my own *impending* death,
'If only I had the magic self of babyhood when I remembered what it was like before I was born, I wouldnt
worry about death now knowing both to be the same
empty dream'—But what will the Rooster say when it
dies, and someone hacks a knife at its fragile chin—And
sweet Hen, she who eats out of Tristessa's paw a globule
of beer, her beak miffling like human lips to chirn up
the milk of the beer—when she dies, sweet hen, Tristessa
who loves her will save her lucky bone and wrap it in
red thread and keep it in her belongings, nevertheless
sweet Mother Hen of our Arc of Noah Night, she the
golden purveyor and reaches so far back you can't find
the egg that prompted her outward through the first
original shell, they'll hack and whack at her tail with
hacksaws and make mincemeat out of her that you run
through an iron grinder turning handle, and would you
wonder why she trembles from fear of punishment too?
And the death of the cat, little dead rat in the gutter
with twisted yickface—I wish I could communicate to all
their combined fears of death the Teaching that I have
heard from Ages of Old, that recompenses all that pain
with soft reward of perfect silent love abiding up and
down and in and out everywhere past, present, and future in the Void unknown where nothing happens and
all simply is what it is. But they know that themselves,
beast and jackal and love woman, and my Teaching of
Old is indeed so old they've heard it long ago before my
time.

I become depressed and I gotta go home. Everyone of us, *born to die*.

BRIGHT EXPLANATION OF the crystal clarity of all the Worlds, I need, to show that we'll all be all right—The measurement of robot machines at this time is rather irrelevant or at any time—The fact that Cruz cooked with a smoky kerosene stove big pottery-fulls of carne meat-general from a whole heifer, bites of veal, pieces of veal tripe and heifer brains and heifer forehead bones . . . this wouldn't ever send Cruz to hell because no one's told her to stop the slaying, and even if someone had, Christ or Buddha or Holy Mohammed, she would still be safe from harm—though by God the heifer ain't—

The little kitty is mewing rapidly for meat—himself a little piece of quivering meat—soul eats soul in the general emptiness.

"STOP COMPLAININ!" I yell to the cat as he raves on the floor and finally jumps and joins us on the bed—The hen is rubbing her long feathery side gently imperceptibly against my shoe–tip and I can barely feel it and look in time to recognize, what a gentle touch it is from Mother Maya—She's the Magic henlayer without origin, the limitless chicken with its head cut off—The

cat is mewing so violently I begin to worry for the
chicken, but no the cat is merely meditating now quietly
over a piece of smell on the floor, and I give the poor
little fellow a whirr a purr on the thin sticky shoulders
with my fingertip—Time to go, I've petted the cat, said
goodbye to God the Dove, and wanta leave the heinous
kitchen in the middle of a vicious golden dream—It's
all taking place in one vast mind, us in the kitchen, I
don't believe a word of it or a substantial atom-empty
hunk of flesh of it, I see right through it, right through
our fleshy forms (hens and all) at the bright amethyst
future whiteness of reality—I am worried but I aint
glad—"Foo," I say, and rooster looks at me, "what z he
mean by *foo!*" and Rooster goes "Cork a Loodle Doo"
a real Sunday morning (which it is now, 2 A M) Squawk
and I see the brown corners of the dream house and
remember my mother's dark kitchen long ago on cold
streets in the other part of the same dream as this cold
present kitchen with its drip-pots and horrors of Indian
Mexico City—Cruz is feebly trying to say goodnight to
me as I prepare to go, I've petted her several times a
pat on the shoulder thinking that's what she wanted at
the right moments and reassured her I loved her and
was on her side "but I had no side of my own," I lie to
myself—I've wondered what Tristessa thought of my
patting her—for awhile I almost thought she was her
mother, one wild moment I divined this: "Tristessa and
El Indio are brother and sister, and this is their Mother,
and they're driving her crazy yakking in the night about

poison and morphine'—Then I realize: "Cruz is a junkey too, uses three gramos a month, she'll be on the same time and antenna of their dream trouble, moaning and groaning they'll all three go through the rest of their lives sick. Addiction and affliction. Like diseases of the mad, insane inside encephilitises of the brain where you knock out your health purposely to hold a feeling of feeble chemical gladness that has no basis in anything but the thinking-mind—Gnosis, they will certainly change me the day they try to lay morphine on me. And on ye."

Though the shot has done me some good and I haven't touched the bottle since, a kind of weary gladness has come over me tinged with wild strength—the morphine has gentlized my concerns but I'd rather not have it for the weakness it brings to my ribs,—I shall have them bashed in—"I don't want no more morphine after this," I vow, and I yearn to get away from all the morphine talk which, after sporadic listens, has finally wearied me.

I get up to go, El Indio will go with me, walk me to the corner, though at first he argues with them as though he wanted to stay or wanted something further—We go out quickly, Tristessa closes the door in back of us, I don't even give her a close look, just a glance as she closes indicating I'll see her later—El Indio and I walk vigorously down the slimey rainy aisles, turn right, and cut out to the market street, I've already commented on his black hat, and now here I am on the street with the famous Black Bastard—I've already laughed and said "You're just like Dave" (Tristessa's ex husband) "you

even wear the black hat" as I'd seen Dave one time, on
Redondas—in the moil and wild of a warm Friday night
with buses parading slowly by and mobs on the sidewalk;
Dave hands the package to his boy, the seller calls the
cop, cop comes running, boy hands it back to Dave, Dave
says 'Okay take it and ron' and tosses it back and boy
hits ledge of a flying bus and hangs in to the crowd with
his loins his body hanging over the street and his arms
rigidly holding the bus door pole, the cops can't catch,
Dave meanwhile has vamoosed into a saloon, removed
his legendary black hat, and sat at the counter with other
men looking straight ahead—cops no find—I had ad-
mired Dave for his guts, now admire El Indio for *his*—
As we come out of the Tristessa tenement he lets loose
a whistle and a shout at a bunch of men on the corner,
we walk right along and they spread and we come up
to the corner and walk right on talking, I've not paid
attention to what he's done, all I wanta do is go straight
home—It's started to drizzle—

"YA VOY DORMIENDO, I go sleep now" says El Indio
putting his palms together at side of his mouth—I say
"Okay" then he makes a further elaborate statement I
think repeating in words what done before by sign, I
fail to acknowledge complete understanding of his new
statement, he disappointedly says "Yo un untiende" (you
dont understand) but I do understand that he wants to

go home and go to bed—"Okay" I say—We shake—We then go through an elaborate smiling routine on the streets of man, in fact on broken cobbles of Redondas—

To reassure him I give him a parting smile and start off but he keeps alertly watching every flicker of my smiler and eyelash, I can't turn away with an arbitrary leer, I want to smile him on his way, he replies by smiles of his own equally elaborate and psychologically corroborative, we swing informations back and forth with crazy smiles of farewell, so much so, El Indio stumbles in the extreme strain of this, over a rock, and throws still a further parting smile of reassurance capping my own, till no end in sight, but we stumble in our opposite directions as though reluctant—which reluctance lasts a brief second, the fresh air of the night hits your newborn solitude and both you and your Indio go off in a new man and the smile, part of the old, is removed, no longer necessita—He to his home, I to mine, why smile about it all night long except in company—The dreariness of the world politely—

I GO DOWN the Wild Street of Redondas, in the rain, it hasn't started increasing yet, I push through and dodge through moils of activity with whores by the hundreds lined up along the walls of Panama Street in front of their crib cells where big Mamacita sits near the cocina pig pottery, as you leave they ask a little for the pig who

also represents the kitchen, the chow, *cocina*,—Taxis are
slanting by, plotters are aiming for their dark, the whores
are nooking the night with their crooking fingers of
Come On, young men pass and give em the once over,
arm in arm in crowds the young Mexicans are Casbah
buddying down their main girl street, hair hanging over
their eyes, drunk, borracho, longlegged brunettes in
tight yellow dresses grab them and sock their pelvics in,
and pull their lapels, and plead—the boys wobble—the
cops down the street pass idly like figures on little wheel-
thucks rolling by invisibly under the sidewalk—One look
through the bar where the children gape and one
through the whoreboy bar of queers where spidery heroes perform whore dances in turtleneck sweaters for
assembled critical elders of 22—look through both holes
and see the eye of the criminal, criminal in heaven.—I
plow through digging the scene, swinging my bag with
the bottle in it, I twist and give the whores a few twisting
looks as I walks, they send me stereotyped soundwaves
of scorn from cussin doorways—I am starving, I start
eating El Indio's sandwich he gave me which at first I'd
sought to refuse so as to leave it for the cat but El Indio
insisted it was a present for me, so I nakedly breast-high
in one delicate hold as I walk along the street—seeing
the sandwich I begin to eat it—finishing it, I start buying
tacos as I run by, any kind, any stand where they yell
"Joven!"—I buy stinking livers of sausages chopped in
black white onions steaming hot in grease that crackles
on the inverted fender of the grille—I munch down on

heats and hotsauce salsas and come to devouring whole
mouthloads of fire and rush along—nevertheless I buy
another one, further, two, of broken cow-meat hacked
on the woodblock, head and all it seems, bits of grit and
gristle, all mungied together on a mangy tortilla and
chewed down with salt, onions, and green leaf—diced—
a delicious sandwich when you get a good stand—The
stands are 1,2,3 in a row a half mile down the street,
tragically lit by candles and dim bulbs and strange lan-
terns, the whole of Mexico a Bohemian Adventure in
the great outdoor plateau night of stones, candle and
mist—I pass Plaza Garibaldi the hot spot of the police,
strange crowds are grouping in narrow streets around
quiet musicians that only later faintly you hear corneting
round the block—Marimbas are drumming in the big
bars—Rich men, poor men, in wide hats mingle—Come
out of swinging doors spitting cigar putts and clapping
big hands over their jock as though they were about to
dive in a cold brook—guilty—Up the side streets dead
buses waddling in the mud holes, spots of fiery yellow
whoredress in the dark, assembled leaners and up
against the wall lovers of the loving Mexican night—
Pretty girls passing, every age, all the comic Gordos and
me turn big heads to watch them, they're too beautiful
to bear—

I rock right by the Post Office, cross the bottom of
Juarez, the Palace of Fine Arts sinking nearby,—yoke
myself to San Juan Letran and fall to hiking up fifteen
blocks of it fast passing delicious places where they make
the churros and cut you hot salt sugar butter bites of

fresh hot donut from the grease basket, that you crunch freshly as you cover the Peruvian night ahead of your enemies on the sidewalk—All kinds of crazy gangs are assembled, chief gleeful leaders getting high on gang leadership wear crazy woollen Scandanavian Ski hats over their zoot paraphenalias and Pachuco haircuts— Other day here I'd passed a gang of children in a gutter their leader dressed as a clown (with nylon stocking over head) and wide rings painted around the eyes, the littler kids have imitated him and attempted similar clown out-fits, the whole thing gray and blackened eyes with white loops, like silks of great racetracks the little gang of Pinocchioan heroes (and Genet) paraphernaliaing on the street curb, an older boy making fun of the Clown Hero "What are you doing clowning, Clown Hero?—There ain't no Heaven anywhere?" "There ain't no Santa Claus of Clown Heroes, mad boy"—Other gangs of semi-hips-ters hide in front of nightclub bars with wronks and noise inside, I fly by with one quick Walt Whitman look at all that file deroll—It starts raining harder, I've got a long way to go walking and pushing that sore leg right along in the gathering rain, no chance no intention what-ever of hailing a cab, the whiskey and the Morphine have made me unruffled by the sickness of the poison in my heart.

WHEN YOU HAVE no more numbers in Nirvana then there won't be such a thing as "numberless" but the crowds on San Juan Letran were like numberless—I say "Count all these sufferings from here to the end of the endless sky which is no sky and see how many you can add together to make a figure to impress the Boss of Dead Souls in the Meat Manufactory in city City CITY everyone of them in pain and born to die, milling in the streets at 2 A M underneath those imponderable skies"— their enormous endlessness, the sweep of the Mexican plateau away from the Moon—living but to die, the sad song of it I hear sometimes on my roof in the Tejado district, rooftop cell, with candles, waiting for my Nirvana or my Tristessa—neither come, at noon I hear "La Paloma" being played on mental radios in the fallways between the tenement windows—the crazy kid next door sings, the dream is taking place right now, the music is so sad, the French horns ache, the high whiney violins and the deberratarra-rabaratarara of the Indian Spanish announcer. Living but to die, here we wait on this shelf, and up in heaven is all that gold open caramel, ope my door—Diamond Sutra is the sky.

I crash along drunkenly and bleakly and hard with kicking feet over the precarious sidewalk slick of vegetable oil Tehuantepec, green sidewalks, swarmed with scumworm invisible but in high—dead women hiding in my hair, passing underneath the sandwich and chair— "You're nuts!" I yell to the crowds in English "You don't know what in a hell you're doing in this eternity bell rope tower swing to the puppeteer of Magadha, Mara the Tempter, insane, . . . And you all eagle and you bea-

gle and you buy—All you bingle you baffle and you lie—
You poor motherin bloaks pourin through the juice
parade of your Main Street Night you don't know that
the Lord has arranged everything in sight." "Including
your death." "And nothing's happening. I am not me,
you are not ye, they unnumbered are not they, and One
Un-Number Self there is no such thing."

I pray at the feet of man, waiting, as they.

As they? As Man? As he? There is no He. There is
only' the unsayable divine word. Which is not a Word,
but a Mystery.

At the root of the Mystery the separation of one world
from another by a sword of light.—

The winners of tonight's ball game in the open mist
outside Tacabatabavac are romping by in the street
swinging their baseball bats at the crowd showing how
great they can hit and the crowd walks unconcernedly
around because they are children not juvenile delin-
quents. They pull their beak baseball hats tight-hawk
down their faces, in the drizzle, tapping their glove they
wonder "Did I make a bad play in the fifth inning? Didn't
I make it up with that *heet* in the seventh inning?"

AT THE END of San Juan Letran is that last series of
bars that end in a ruined mist, fields of broken adobe,
no bums hidden, all wood, Gorky, Dank, with sewers
and puddles, ditches in the street five feet deep with

water in the bottom—powdery tenements against the
light of the nearby city—I watch the final sad bar-doors,
where flashes of women golden shining lace behinds I
can see and feel like flying in yet like a bird in flight
twist on. Kids are in the doorway in goof suits, the band
is wailing a chachacha inside, everybody's knee is knocking to bend as they pop and wail with the mad music,
the whole club is rocking, *down*, an American Negro
walking with me would have said "These cats are stoning
themselves on some real hip kicks, they are goofing all
the time, they wail, they spend all the time knocking and
knocking for that *bread*, for that *girl*, they're up in against
the doorways, man, wailing all—you know? They don't
know when to stop. It's like Omar Khayyam, I wonder
what the vintners buy, one half so precious, as what they
sell." (My boy Al Damlette.)

I TURN OFF at these last bars and it really starts raining
hard and I walk fast as I can and come to a big puddle
and jump out of it all wet and jump right in again and
cross it—The morphine prevents me from feeling the
wet, my skin and limbs are numb,—like a kid when he
goes skating in winter, falls through ice, runs home with
skates under his arm so he won't catch cold, I kept plow-
ing through the Pan American rain and above is the
gigantic roar of a Pan American Airplane coming in to
land at Mexico City Airport with passengers from New

York looking for to find the other end of dreams. I look up into the drizzle and watch their tail firespark—you won't find me landing over great cities and all I do is clutch the side of the seat and wobble as the air pilot expertly leads us into a tremendous flaming crash against the side of warehouses in the slum district of Old Indian Town—what? with all them rat tat tans with revolvers in their pockets pushing through my foggy bones looking for something made of gold, and then rats gnaw ya.

I'd rather walk than ride the airplane, I can fall on the ground flat on my face and die that way.—With a watermelon under my arm. *Mira.*

I COME UP gorgeous Orizaba Street (after crossing wide muddy parks near Ciné Mexico and the dismal trolley street called after dismal General Obregon in the rainy night, with roses in his mother's hair—) Orizaba Street has a magnificent fountain and pool in a green park at a round O-turn in residential splendid shape of stone and glass and old grills and scrolly worly lovely majesties that when looked at by the moon blend with magic inner Spanish gardens of an architecture (if architecture you will) designed for lovely nights at home. Andalusian in intention.

The fountain is not spraying water at 2 A M and as though it would have to, in the driving rain, and me rolling by there sitting on my railroad switchblock pass-

ing over pinking sparking switches on tracks of under-
neath-the-earth like the cops on the little whorestreet 35
blocks back and way downtown—

It's the dismal rainy night caught up with me—my
hair is dripping water, my shoes are slopping—but I
have my jacket on, and it is soaking on the outside—but
it is rain repellent—"Why I bought it back in the Rich-
mond Bank" I'm tellin heroes about it later, in a littlekid
dream.—I run on home, walking past the bakery where
they don't at 2 A M anymore make latenight donuts,
twisters taken out of ovens and soaked in syrup and sold
to you through the bakery window for two cents apiece
and I'd buy baskets of them in my younger days—closed
now, rainy night Mexico City of the present contains no
roses and no fresh hot donuts and it's bleak. I cross the
last street, slow down and relax letting out breath and
stumbling on my muscles, now I go in, death or no death,
and sleep the sweet sleep of white angels.

But my door is locked, my street door, I have no key
for it, all lights are out, I stand there dripping in the
rain with no place to dry up and sleep—I see there's a
light in Old Bull Gaines' window and I go over and
amazedly look in, just see his golden curtain, I realize
"If I can't get in my own place then I'll just knock on
Bull's window and sleep in his easy chair." Which I do,
knocking, and he comes out of the dark establishment
of about 20 people and in his bathrobe walks through
the little bit of rain between building and the door—
comes and snaps open the iron door. I go in after him—
"Can't go in my own place" I say—He wants to know

what Tristessa said about tomorrow, when they get more stuff from the Black Market, the Red Market, the Indian Market—So it's alright with Old Bull I sleep and stay in his room—"Till the street door is opened at 8 A M" I add, and suddenly decide to curl up on the floor with a flimsy coverlet, which, instantly as done, is like a bed of soft fleece and I lay there divine, legs all tired and clothes partly wet (am wrapped in Old Bull's big towel robe like a ghost in a Turkish bath) and the whole journey in the rain done, all I have to do is lie dreaming on the floor. I curl up and start sleeping. In the middle of the night now, with the small yellowbulb on, and rain crashing outside, Old Bull Gaines has closed shutters tight, is smoking cigarette after cigarette and I can't breathe in the room and he's coughing "Ke-he!" the dry junkey cough, like a protest, like yelling *Wake Up!*—he lies there, thin, emaciated, long nosed, strangely handsome and gray haired and lean and mangy 22 in his derelict worldling ("student of souls and cities" he calls himself) decapitated and bombed out by morphine frame—Yet all the guts in the world. He starts munching on candy, I lay there waking up realizing that Old Bull is munching on candy noisily in the night—All the sides to this dream—Annoyed, I glance anxiously around and see him myorking and monching on condy after condy, what a preposterous thing to do at 4 A M in your bed—Then at 4:30 he's up and boiling down a couple of capsules of morphine in a spoon,—you see him, after the shot has been sucked in and siphoned out, with big glad tongue licking so he can spit on the blackened bottom of the spoon and rub it clean and silver with a piece of paper, using, to really polish the spoon, a pinch of ashes—And he lays back, feeling it a little, it takes ten minutes, a muscle bang,—by about twenty minutes he might feel alright—if not, there he is rustling in his drawer waking me up again, he's looking for his goof-balls—"So he can sleep."

So *I* can sleep. But no. Immediately he wants another jolt of some kind, he ups and opes his drawer and pulls out a tube of codeine pills and counts out ten and pops that in with a slug of cold coffee from his old cup that sits on the chair by the bed—and he endures in the night, with the light on, and lights further cigarettes—At some time or other, around dawn, he falls asleep—I get up after some reflections at 9 or 8, or 7, and quickly put my wet clothes on to rush upstairs to my warm bed and dry clothes—Old Bull is sleeping, he finally made it, Nirvana, he's snoring and he's out, I hate to wake him up but he'll have to lock himself in, with his bolt and slider—It's gray outside, rain has finally stopped after heaviest surge at dawn. 40,000 families were flooded out in the Northwestern part of Mexico City that storm. Old Bull, far from floods and storms with his needles and his powders beside the bed and cottons and eyedroppers and paraphernalias—"When you got morphine, you dont need anything else, me boy," he says to me in the daytime all combed and high sitting in his easy chair with papers the picture of glad health—"Madame Poppy, I call her. When you've got Opium you've got all you need.—All that good *O* goes down in your veins and you feel like singing Hallelujah!" And he laughs. "Bring me Grace Kelly on this chair, Morphine on that chair, I'll take Morphine."

"Ava Gardner *too*?"

"Ava GVavna and all the bazotzkas in all the countries so far—if I can have my M in the morning and my M in the afternoon and my M in the evening before going to bed, I dont even need to know what time it is on the City Hall Clock—" He tells me all this and more nodding vigorously and sincerely. His jaw quivers with emotion. "Why for krissakes if I had no junk I'd be bored to death, I'd die of *boredom*" he complains, almost crying—"I read Rimbaud and Verlaine, I know what I'm talking about—Junk is the only thing I want—You've never been junksick, you don't know what it's like—Boy when you wake up in the morning sick and take a good bang, boy, that feels good." I can picture myself and Tristessa waking up in our nuptial madbed of blankets and dogs and cats and canaries and dots of whoreplant in the coverlet and naked shoulder to shoulder (under the gentle eyes of the Dove) she shoots me in or I shoot myself in a big bang of waterycolored poison straight into the flesh of your arm and into your system which it instantly proclaims *its*—you feel the weak fall of your body to the disease in the solution—but never having been junksick, I don't know the horror of the disease—A story Old Bull could tell much better than I—

HE LETS ME out, but not until he's muttered and sputtered out of bed—holding his pajamas and bathrobe, pushing in his belly where it hurts, where some kind of hernia cave-in annoys him,—poor sick fella, almost 60 years old and hanging on to his diseases without bothering anybody—Born in Cincinnati, brought up in the Red River Steamboats. (redlegged? his legs as white as snow)—

I see that it's stopped raining and I'm thirsty and have drunk Old Bull's two cups of water (boiled, and kept in a jar)—I go across the street in my damp sopping shoes and buy an ice-cold Spur Cola and gobble it down on my way to my room—The skies are opening up, there might be sunshine in afternoon, the day is almost wild and Atlantican, like a day at sea off the coast of the Firth of Scotland—I yell imperial flags in my thoughts and rush up the two flights to my room, the final flight a ricket of iron tin-spans creaking and cracking on nails and full of sand, I get on the hard adobe floor of the roof, the Tejado, and walk on slippery little puddles around the air of the courtyard rail only two foot high so you can just easily fall down three flights and crack your skull on tile Espaniala floors where Americans gnash and fight sometimes in raucous parties early in the twilight of the morning,—I could fall, Old Bull almost fell over when he lived on the roof a month, the

children sit on the soft stone of the 2 foot rail and goof
and talk, all day running around the thing and skidding
and I never like to watch—I come to my room around
two curves of the Hole and unlock my padlock which
is hooked to decaying halfout nails (one time left the
room open and unattended all day)—I go in and jam
the door in the rain damp wood and rain has swollen
the wood and the door barely tightens at the top—I get
in my dry hobo pants and two big hobo shirts and go
to bed with thick socks on and finish the Spur and lay
it on the table and say "Ah" and wipe the back of my
mouth and look awhile at holes in my door showing the
outside Sunday morning sky and I hear churchbells
down Orizaba lane and people are going to church and
I'm going to sleep and I'll make up for it later, goodnight.

"BLESSED LORD, THOU lovedest all sentient life."
   Why do I have to sin and do the sign of the Cross?
   "Not one of the vast accumulation of conceptions from
beginningless time, through the present and into the
never ending future, not one of them is graspable."
   It's the old question of "Yes life's not real" but you
see a beautiful woman or something you can't get away
from wanting because it is there in front of you—This
beautiful woman of 28 standing in front of me with her
fragile body ("I put thees in my neck [a dicky] so nobody
look and see my beautiful body," she thinks she jokes,

not regarding herself as beautiful) and that face so expressive of the pain and loveliness that went no doubt
into the making of this fatal world,— a beautiful sunrise,
that makes you stop on the sands and gaze out to sea
hearing Wagner's Magic Fire Music in your thoughts—
the fragile and holy countenance of poor Tristessa, the
tremulous bravery of her little junk-racked body that a
man could throw up in the air ten feet—the bundle of
death and beauty—all pure Form standing in front of
me, all the racks and tortures of sexual beauty, the breast,
the limb of the middle body, the whole huggable mess
of a woman some of them even though 6 feet high you
can slumber on their bellies in the night like a nap on
a dreaming bankside of a woman—Like Goethe at 80,
you know the futility of love and you shrug—You shrug
away the warm kiss, the tongue and lips, the tug at the
thin waist, the whole warm floating thing against you
held tight—the little woman—for which rivers flow and
men fall down stepladders—The thin cold long brown
fingers of Tristessa, slow, and casual and lazy, like the
meeting of lips—The Tristessa Spanish Night of her
deep love hole, the bullfights in her dreams of you, the
lazy rainy rose against the idle cheek—And all the con-
comitant lovelinesses of a lovely woman a young man
in a far-off country should yearn to stay for—I was trav-
eling around in circles in North America in many a gray
tragedy.

I STAND LOOKING at Tristessa, she's come to visit me in my room, she won't sit down, she stands and talks— in the candle light she is excited and eager and beautiful and radiant—I sit down on the bed, looking down on the stony floor, while she talks—I don't even listen to what she's saying, about junk, Old Bull, how she's tired— "I go to the do it to-*morra*—TO-MORRAR—" she taps to emphasize me with her hand, so I have to say "Yeh Yeh go ahead" and she goes on with her story, which I don't understand—I just can't look at her for fear of thoughts I'll get—But she takes care of all of that for me, she says "Yes, we are in pain—" I say "La Vida es dolor" (life is pain), she agrees, she says life is love too. "When you got one million pesos I dont care how many, they dont move"—she says, indicating my paraphernalia of leather-covered scriptures and Sears Roebuck enve- lopes with stamps and airmail envelopes inside—as though I had a million pesos hiding in time in my floor— "A million pesos does not move—but when you got the friend, the friend give it to you in the bed" she says, legs spread a little, pumping with her loins at the air in the direction of my bed to indicate how much better a human being is than a million paper pesos—I think of the inex- pressible tenderness of receiving this holy friendship from the sacrificial sick body of Tristessa and I almost feel crying or grabbing her and kissing her—A wave of

loneliness passes over me, remembering past loves and
bodies in beds and the unbeatable surge when you go
into your beloved deep and the whole world goes with
you—Though we know that Mara the Tempter is evil,
his fields of temptation are innocent—How could Tristessa, rousing passion in me, have anything to do, except
as a field of merit or a dupe of innocence or a material
witness to my murderous lust, how could she be blamed
and how could she be sweeter than standing there explaining my love directly with her pantomiming thighs.
She's high, she keeps trying at the lapel of her kimono
(underneath's a slip that shows) and trying to attach it
unattachably to an inexistent button of the coat. I look
into her eyes deep, meaning "Would you be my friend
like that?" and she looks straight at me pools of neither
this or that, her combination of reluctance to break her
personal disgust covenant moreover lodged in the Virgin
Mary, and her love of wish-for-me, makes her as mysterious as the Tathagata whose form is described as being
as inexistent, rather as inscrutable as the direction in
which a put-out fire has gone. I can't get a yes or no out
of her eyes for the time I allot to them. Very nervous,
I sit, stand, sit, she stands explaining further things. I
am amazed by the way her skin wrinkles O so sensitively
down the bridge of her nose in even clean lines, and her
little laugh of delight that comes so rarely and so's lit-
tlegirlish, child of glee,—It's all my own sin if I make a
play for her.

I WANT TO take her in both hands by the waist and pull her slowly close with a few choice words of sudden endearment like "Mi gloria angela" or "Mi whichever it is" but I have no language to cover my embarrassment— Worst of all, would it be, to have her push me aside and say "No, no, no" like disappointed mustachio'd heroes in French movies being turned out by the little blonde who is the brakeman's wife, by a fence, in smoke, midnight, in the French railroad yards, and I turn away big pained loverface and apologize,—going away thence with the sensation that I have a beastly streak in me I didn't notice, conceptions common to all young lovers and old. I don't want to disgust Tristessa—It would horrify me to cause her ruinous fleshpetal tender secrets and have her wake up in the morning lodged against the back of some unwelcome man who loves by night and sleeps it off, and wakes up blearing to shave and by his very presence causes consternation where before there was absolute perfect purity of nobody.

But what I've missed when I don't get that friend lunge of the lover's body, coming right at me, all mine, but it was a slaughterhouse for meat and all you do is bend to wreak havocs in somethings-gotta-give of girlihood.—When Tristessa was 12 years old suitors twisted her arm in the sun outside the mother's cooking door— I've seen it a million times, in Mexico the young men

want the young girls—Their birthrate is terrific—They
turn em out wailing and dying by the golden tons in vats
of semiwinery messaferies of oy Ole Tokyo birthcrib.—
I lost track of my thought there,—

Yes, the thighs of Tristessa and the golden flesh all
mine, what am I a Caveman? Am a Caveman.

Caveman buried deep under ground.

It would just be the coronna of her cheeks pulsing to
mouth, and my rememberance of her splendid eyes, like
sitting in a box the lovely latest in France enters the
crashing orchestra and I turn to Monsieur next to me
whispering "She is *splendide*, non?"—With Johnny Walker
Scotch in my tuxedo coatpocket.

I stand up. I must see her.

POOR TRISTESSA IS swaying there explaining all her
troubles, how she hasn't got enough money, she's sick,
she'll be sick in the morning and in the look of her eye
I caught perhaps the gesture of a shadow of acceptance
of the idea of me as a lover—Only time I ever saw Tristessa cry, was when she was junk sick on the edge of Old
Bull's bed, like a woman in the back pew of a church in
daily novena she dabs at her eyes—She points to the sky
again, "If my friend dont pay me back," looking at me
straight, "my Lord pay me back—*more*" and I can feel
the spirit enter the room as she stands, waiting with her
finger pointed up, on her spread legs, confidently, for

her Lord to pay her back—"So I geev every-things I have to my friend, and eef he doan pay me back"—she shrugs—"my Lord pay me back"—standing alert again—"*More*" and as the spirit swims around the room I can tell the effective mournful horror of it (her reward is so thin) now I see radiating from the crown of her head innumerable hands that have come from all ten quarters of the Universe to bless her and pronounce her Bodhisat for saying and knowing that so well.

Her Enlightenment is perfect,—"And we are nothing, you and me"—she pokes at my chest, "Jew—Jew—" (Mexican saying "You")"—and me"—pointing at herself—"We are *nothing*. Tomorrar we may be die, and so we are nothing—" I agree with her, I feel the strangeness of that truth, I feel we are two empty phantoms of light or like ghosts in old haunted-house stories diaphanous and precious and white and not-there,—She says "I know you want to sleep."

"No no" I say, seeing she wants to leave—

"I go to it sleep, early in the mawnins I go get see for the mans and I get the morfina and com bock for Old Bool"—and since we are *nada*, nothing, I forget what she said about friends all lost in the beauty of her strange intelligent imagery, every bit true—"She's an Angel," I think secretly, and escort her to the door with movement of arm as she leans to the door talking to go out—We are careful not to touch each other—I tremble, once I jumped a mile when her fingertip hit my knee in conversations, at chairs—the first afternoon I'd seen her, in dark glasses, in the sunny afternoon window, by a candle light lit for kicks, sick kicks of life, smoking, beautiful, like the Owner Damsel of Las Vegas, or the Revolutionary Heroine of Marlon Brando Zapata Mexico— with Culiacan heroes and all—That's when she got me— In afternoon space of gold the look, the sheer beauty, like silk, the children giggling, me blushing, at guy's house, where we first found Tristessa and started all this—Sympaticus Tristessa with her heart a gold gate, I'd first dug to be an evil enchantress—I'd run across a Saint in Modern Mexico and here I was fantasizing dreams away about foreordained orders for nothing and necessary betrayals—the betrayal of the old father when he entices by ruse the three little crazy kids screaming and playing in the burning house, "I'll give each one your favorite cart," out they come running for the carts, he gives them the High Incomparable Great Cart of the Single Vehicle White Bullock which they're too young to appreciate—with that greatcart command, he'd made me an offer—I look at Tristessa's leg and decide to avoid the issue of fate and rest beyond heaven.

I play games with her fabulous eyes and she longs to be in a monastery.

"LEAVE TRISTESSA ALONE" I say, anyway, like I'd say "Leave the kitty alone, don't hurt it"—and I open her the door, so we can go out, at midnight, from my

room—In my hand I stumble-awkwardly hold big railroad brakeman lantern to her feet as we descend the
perilous needless to say steps, she'd almost tripped coming up, she moaned and she groaned coming up, she
smiled and minced with her hand on her skirt going
down, with that majestical lovely slowness of woman, like
a Chinese Victoria.

"We are nothing."

"Tomorrow we may be die."

"We are nothing."

"You and Me."

I politely lead all the way down by light and lead her
out to street where I hail her a white taxi for her home.

Since beginningless time and into the never-ending
future, men have loved women without telling them,
and the Lord has loved them without telling, and the
void is not the void because there's nothing to be empty
of.

Art there, Lord Star?—Diminished is the drizzle that
broke my calm.

PART TWO

A Year Later . . .

DIMINISH'D NEVER IS the drizzle that broke no calm—I didnt tell her I loved her but when I left Mexico I began to think on her and then I began to tell her I loved her in letters, and almost did, and she wrote too, pretty Spanish letters, saying I was sweet, and please hurry back—I hurried back too late, I should have come back in the Spring, almost did, had no money, just touched the border of Mexico and felt that vomity feeling of Mexico—went on to California and lived in a shack with young monk Buddhist type visitors every day and went north to Desolation Peak and spent a summer surling in the Wilderness, eating and sleeping alone—said, "Soon I go back, to the warm arms of Tristessa"—but waited too long.

O Lord, why have you done this to your angel-selves, this blight life, this ugh raggedy crap scene full of puke and thieves and dying?—couldnt you have placed us in a dismal heaven where all was glad anyhow?—Art thou Masochist, Lord, art thou Indian Giver, art thou Hater?

Finally I was back in Bull's room after a four thousand mile voyage from the mountain peak near Canada, a terrible enough trip in itself, not worth moot herein— and he went out and got her.

Already he'd warned me: "I dont know what's the matter with her, she's changed in the past two weeks, the *past week* even—"

"Is that because she knew I was coming?" I thought darkly—

"She throws fits and hits me over the head with coffee cups and loses my money and falls in the street—"

"What's the *matter* with her?"

"Goofballs—I told her not to take too many—You know it takes an old junkey with many years of experience to know how to handle sleeping pills,—she wont listen, she dont know how to use em, three, four, sometimes five, once twelve, it's not the same Tristessa—What I wanta do is *marry* her and get my citizenship, see, you think that's a good idea?—After all, she's my life, I'm her life—"

I could see Old Bull had fallen in love—with a woman not named Morphina.

"I never touch her—it's just a marriage of convenience—you know what I mean—I cant be getting stuff on the black market myself, I dont know how, I need her and she needs my money."

Bull got $150 a month from a trust fund established by his father before he died—his father had loved him, and I could know why, for Bull is a sweet and tender person, though just a little of the con man, for years in New York he supported his junk habit by stealing about $30 every day, twenty years—He'd been in jail a few times when they'd found him with wrong merchandise— In jail he was always the librarian, he is a great scholar, in many ways, with a marvelous interest in history and anthropology and of all things French Symbolist poetry, Mallarmé above all—I'm not talking of the other Bull who is the great writer who wrote "Junkey"—This is another Bull, older, almost 60, I wrote poems in his room all last summer when Tristessa was *mine, mine*, and I wouldnt take her—I had some silly ascetic or celibacious notion that I must not touch a woman—My touch might have saved her—

Now too late—

He brings her home and right away I see something is wrong—She comes tottering in on his arm and gives a weak (thank God for that) smile and holds out her arm rigidly, I dont know what to do but hold her arm up, "What's the matter with Tristessa is she sick?"

"All last month she was paralyzed down one whole leg and her arms were covered with cysts, O she was an awful sick girl last month"

"What's the matter with her now?"

"Shh—let her sit down—"

Tristessa is holding me and slowly levels her sweet brown cheek against mine, with a rare smile, and I'm playing the befuddled American almost consciously—

Look, I'll save her yet—

TROUBLE IS, WHAT would I do with her once I'd won her?—it's like winning an angel in hell and you are then entitled to go down with her to where it's worse or maybe there'll be light, some, down there, maybe it's me's crazy—

"She's going crazy," says Bull, "those goofballs'll do it to everybody, to you, anybody I dont care who."

In fact Bull himself took too many two nights later and proved it—

The problem of junkies, narcotic addicts bless their soul, bless their quiet thoughtful souls, is to get it—On all sides they're balked, they are continually unhappy— "If the government gave me enough morphine every day I would be completely happy and I would be completely willing to work as a male nurse in a hospital—I even sent the government my ideas on the subject, in a letter in 1938 from Lexington, how to solve the narcotic problem, by putting junkies to work, with their daily doses, cleaning the subways, anything—as long as they get their medicine they're all right, just like any other sick people—It's like alcoholics, they need medicine—"

I cant remember everything that happened except for last night so fateful, so horrible, so sad and mad—Better to do it that way, why build up?

IT ALL STARTED out with Bull being out of morphine, sick, a little too many goofballs he'd taken (secanols) to make up for the morphine lack and so he is acting like a baby, sloppy, like senile, not quite as bad as the night he slept in my bed on the roof because Tristessa had gone mad and was breaking everything in his room and hitting him and falling on the floor right on her head, goofballs she bought in a drugstore, Bull would give her no more—The anxious landladies are hovering at the door thinking we're beating her up but she's beating us up—

The things she said to me, what she really thought of me, now came out, a year later, a year too late, and all I should have done was *tell her* I loved her—She accused me of being a filthy teahead, she ordered me out of Bull's room, she tried to hit me with a bottle, she tried to take my tobacco pouch and keep it, I had to struggle with her—Bull and I hid the bread knife under the rug— She just sits there on the floor like an idiot baby, doodling with objects—She accuses me of trying to smoke marijuana out of my tobacco pouch but it is only Bull Durham tobacco for my roll-me-owns because commercial cigarettes have a chemical in them to keep them firm that damaged my susceptible phlebitic veins and arteries—

So Bull is afraid she'll kill him in the night, we cant get her out, previously (a week ago) he'd called cops and

ambulances and even they wouldnt get her out, Mexico—So he comes sleep in my new room bed, with clean
sheets, forgets that he's already taken two goofballs and
takes two more and thereupon goes blind, cant find his
cigarettes, gropes and knocks down everything, pees in
the bed, spills coffee I bring him, I have to sleep on the
floor of stone among bedbugs and cockroaches, I revile
him all night poutingly: "Look what you're doing to my
nice clean bed"

"I cant help it—I gotta find another cap—Is this a
cap?" He holds up a matchstick and thinks it's a capsule
of morphine. "Bring me your spoon"—He's going to
boil it down and shoot it—Lord—In the morning at gray
time he finally leaves and goes down to his room, stumbling with all his things including a Newsweek he could
have never read—I dump his cans of pee in the toilet,
it's all pure blue like the blue Sir of Joshua Reynolds,
I think: "MY GOD, he's gotta be dying!" but turns out
they were cans of washing blueing—Meanwhile Tristessa
has slept and feels better and somehow they stumble
around and get their shots and next day she returns
tapping in Bull's window, pale and beautiful, no more
an Aztec witch, and apologizes sweetly—

"She'll be back on goofballs in a week," says Bull—
"But I'm not giving her any more"—He swallows one
himself—

"Why do *you* take em!" I yell.

"Because I know how, I've been a junkey for forty
years"

Comes then the fateful night—

I've already finally in a cab and once on the street told Tristessa I love her—"Yo te amo"—No reply—She lies to Bull and tells him I propositioned her saying "You've slept with a lot of men, why not sleep with me"—No such thing I ever said, just "Yo te amo"—Because I do love her—But what to do with her—She never used to lie before the goofballs—In fact she used to pray and go to church—

I've given up on Tristessa and this afternoon, Bull sick, we get a cab and go down into the slums to find El Indio (the Black Bastard he's called in the trade), who always has something—It's always been my secret hunch that El Indio loves Tristessa too—He has beautiful grown daughters, he lies in a bed behind flimsy curtains with the door wide open to the world, high on M, his elder wife sits anxiously in a chair, ikons burn, arguments take place, groans, all under the endless Mexican skies—We come to his pad and his old wife tells us she is his wife (we didnt know) and he's not in so we sit on the stone steps of the crazy courtyard full of screaming children and drunks and women with wash and banana peels you'd think, and wait there—Bull is so sick he has to go home—Tall, humped, wizard cadaver-like he goes, leaving me sitting drunk on the stone drawing pictures of the children in my little notebook—

Then out comes a host of some kind, a portly friendly man, with a waterglass of pulque, two glasses, he insists I chugalug mine with his, I do, bang, down, the cactus

juice dripping from our lips, he beats me to the draw—
Women laugh—There's a big kitchen—He brings me
more—I drink and draw the children—I offer money
for the pulque but they wont take it—It starts to grow
dark in the courtyard—

I've already swallowed a fifth of wine on the way down,
it's one of my drinking days, I've been bored and sad
and lost—too, for three days I've been painting and
drawing with pencil, chalk and watercolors (my first for-
mal try) and I'm exhausted—I've sketched a little
bearded Mexican artist in his roof hut and he tore the
picture out of the big notebook to keep it—We drank
tequila in the morning and drew each other—Of me he
drew a kind of tourist sketch showing how young and
handsome and American I am, I dont understand (he
wants me to buy it?)—Of him I draw a terrible apocalyptic black bearded face, also his body tinily twisted on
the edge of the couch, O heaven and posterity will judge
all this art, whatever it is—So I'm drawing one particular
little boy who wont stand still then I start drawing the
Virgin Madonna—

More fellows appear and they invite me into a big
room where a big white table is covered with pulque
cups and on the floor open urns of it—Amazing the
faces in there—I think "I'll have a good time and meanwhile I'm right on El Indio's doorstep and I'll catch him
for Bull when he comes home—and Tristessa'll come
too—"

Borracho, we drain big cups of cactus juice and there's
an old singer with guitar with his young disciple boy

with thick sensitive lips and a big fat hostess woman like out of Rabelais and Rembrandt Middle Ages who sings— The leader of this huge gang of fifteen appears to be Pancho Villa at the table end, red clay face, perfectly round and jocund, but Mexican owlish, with crazy eyes (I think) and a wild red checked shirt and like always ecstatically happy—But beside him other more sinister lieutenants of some sort, to them I look downtable right dead in the eye and toast and even ask "Que es la vida? What is life?"—(to prove I'm philosophical and smart)— Meanwhile a man in a blue suit and blue hat appears the most friendly, he beckons me to the toilet for a swaying talk over urine—He locks the door—His eyes are sunken deep in pudgy battered W.C. Fields sockets— "sockets" too clean a word—but a wicked pair of funny eyes, also a hypnotist, I keep staring at him, I keep *liking* him—I like him so much that when he takes my wallet out and counts my money I laugh, I fiddle a little bit trying to get it back, he holds off counting—Others are trying to get in the toilet—"This is Mexico!" says he. "We stay here if we like"—When he hands me back my wallet I see my money's still in it but I swear on the Bible on God on Buddha on all that was supposed to be holy, in real life there was no more money in that wallet (wallet, shwallet, just a leather foldcase for travelers checks)— He leaves me *some* money because later I give twenty pesos to a big fat guy and tell him to go out and get some marijuana for the whole group—He too keeps taking me to the toilet for earnest confabs, somehow my dark glasses disappear—

Finally Blue Hat in front of everybody simply snatches my notebook out of my (Bull's) coat, like a joke, pencil and all, and slips it in his own coat and stares at me, wicked and funny—I really cant help laughing but then I do say "Come on, come on, give me back my poems" and I reach into his coat and he twists away, and I reach again and he wont—I turn to the most distinguished-looking man there, in fact the only one, who is sitting next to me, "Will you undertake the responsibility of getting my poems back."

He says he will, without understanding what I'm saying, but I drunkedly assume he will—Meanwhile in a blind dazzle of ecstasy I throw fifty pesos on the floor to prove something—Later I throw two pesos on the floor saying "It's for the music"—They end up feeding that to the two musicians but I'm too proud after reconsideration to start looking around for my 50 pesos too but you will see that this is just a case of wanting to be robbed, a strange kind of exultation and drunken power, "I dont care about money, I am the King of the world, I will lead your little revolutions myself"—This I begin to work on by making friends with Pancho Villa, and brother there's a lot of knocking of cups and arm-around-chugalugs down, and song—And by this time I'm too stupid to check my wallet but every cent is gone— I take great pride meanwhile in showing how I appreciate the music, I even drum on the table—Finally I go out with Fat Boy to talk in the toilet and as we're coming out here comes a strange woman up the steps, unearthly

and pale, slow, majestic, neither young nor old, I cant
help staring at her and even when I realize it's Tristessa
I keep staring and wondering at this strange woman and
it seems that she has come to save me but she's only
coming for a shot from El Indio (who, by the way, had
by now, on his own accord, gone to Bull's two miles
away)—I leave the gay gang of thieves and follow my
love.

She is wearing a long dirty dress and a shawl and her
face is pale, little rings under the eyes, that thin patri-
cian slowly hawked nose, those luscious lips, those sad
eyes—and the music of her voice, the complaint of her
song, when she talks in Spanish to others . . .

AH SACRISTI—the sad mutilated blue Madonna, is
Tristessa, and for me to keep saying that I love her is
a bleeding lie—She hates me and I hate her, make no
bones about it—I hate her because she hates me, no
other reason—She hates me because I dont know, I guess
I was too pious last year—She keeps yelling "*I dunt care!*"
and hits us over the head and goes out and sits on the
curb in the street and doodles and sways—Nobody dares
approach the woman with her head between her knees—
Tonight though I can see she's alright, quiet, pale, walking straight, coming up the stone steps of the thieves—
El Indio aint in, we go down again—I had already
twice visited El Indio's to check on him, not there, but

his brown daughter with the beautiful brown sad eyes
staring out into the night as I question her, "Non, non,"
is all she can say, she is staring at some fixed point in
the garbage of the sky, so all I do is stare at her eyes
and I have never seen such a girl—Her eyes seem to say
"I love my father even tho he takes narcoticas, but please
dont come here, leave him alone"—

Tristessa and I go down to the slippery garbage street
of dull brown cokestand lights and distant dim blue and
rose neons (like rubbed chalk crayon) of Santa Maria de
Redondas, where we hook up with poor bedraggled wild
looking Cruz and start off somewhere—

I have my arm around Tristessa's waist and walk sadly
with her—Tonight she doesnt hate me—Cruz always
liked me and still does—In the past year she has caused
poor old Bull every kind of trouble with her drunk she-
nanigans—O there's been pulque and vomiting in the
streets and groans under heaven, spattered angel wings
covered with the pale blue dirt of heaven—Angels in
hell, our wings huge in the dark, the three of us start
off, and from the Golden Eternal Heaven bends God
blessing us with his face which I can only describe as
being infinitely sorry (compassionate), that is, infinite
with understanding of suffering, the sight of that Face
would make you cry—I've seen it, in a vision, it will cancel
all in the end—No tears, just the lips, O I can show
you!—No woman could be that sad, God is like a man—
It's all a blank how we go up the street to some small
narrow dark street where two women are sitting with

steaming cauldrons of some kind, or steamcups, where we sit on wood crates, I with my head on Tristessa's shoulder, Cruz at my feet, and they give me a drink of hot punch—I look in my wallet, no more money, I tell Tristessa, she pays for the drinks, or talks, or runs the whole show, maybe she's the leader of the gang of thieves even—

The drinks dont help much, it's getting late, towards dawn, the chill of the high plateau gets into my little sleeveless shirt and loose sports coat and shino pants and I start shivering uncontrollably—Nothing helps, drink after drink, nothing helps—

Two young Mexican cats attracted by Tristessa come and stand there drinking and talking all night, both have mustaches, one of them is very short with a round baby face with pear-like cheeks—The other is taller, with wings of newspaper stuck somehow in his jacket to protect him from the cold—Cruz just stretches out right in the road in her topcoat and goes to sleep, head on the ground, on the stone—A cop arrests somebody at the head of the alley, we around the little candle flames and steampots watch without much interest—At one point Tristessa kisses me gently on the lips, the softest, just-touchingest kiss in the world—Aye, and I receive it with amazement—I've made up my mind to stay with her and sleep where she sleeps, even if she sleeps in a garbage can, in a stone cell with rats—But I keep shivering, no amount of wrapping in can do it, for a year now I've been spending every night in my sleeping bag and I'm

no longer inured to ordinary dawn chills of the earth—
At one point I fall right off the crate I occupy with
Tristessa, land in the sidewalk, stay there—Other times
I'm up haranguing long mysterious conversations with
the two cats—What on earth are they trying to say and
do?—Cruz sleeps in the street—

Her hair hangs out all black across the road, people
step over her.—It's the end.

Dawn comes gray.

PEOPLE START PASSING to go to work, soon the pale
light begins to reveal the incredible colors of Mexico,
the pale blue shawls of women, the deep purple shawls,
the lips of people faintly roseate in general aubeal blue—

"What we waiting for? Where we goin?" I'd kept
asking—

"I go get my shot," she says—gets me another hot
punch, which goes down shivering through me—One
of the ladies is asleep, the dealer with ladle is beginning
to get sore because apparently I've drank more than
Tristessa paid or the two cats or something—

Many people and carts pass—

"Vamonos," says Tristessa getting up, and we wake
up ragged Cruz and waver a minute standing, and go
off in the streets—

Now you can see to the ends of the streets, no more

garbanzo darkness, it's all pale blue churches and pale
people and pink shawls—We move along and come to
rubbly fields and cross and come to a settlement of adobe
huts—

It's a village in the city by itself—

We meet a woman and go into a room and I figure
we'll finally sleep in here but the two beds are loaded
with sleepers and wakers, we just stand there talking,
leave and go down the alley past waking-up doors—
Everybody curious to see the two ragged girls and the
raggedy man, stumbling like a slow team in the dawn—
The sun comes up orange over piles of red brick and
plaster dust somewhere, it's the wee North America of
my Indian Dreams but now I'm too gone to realize anything or understand, all I wanta do is sleep, next to
Tristessa—She in her skimpy pink dress, her little breast-
less body, her thin shanks, her beautiful thighs, but I'm
willing to just sleep but I'd like to hold her and stop
shivering under some vast dark brown Mexican Blanket
with Cruz too, on the other side, to chaperone, I just
wanta stop this insane wandering in the streets—

No soap, at the end of the village, in the final house,
beyond which is fields of dumps and distant Church tops
and the bleary city, we go in—

What a scene! I jump to rejoice to see a huge bed—
"We're coming to sleep here!"

But in the bed is a big fat woman with black hair, and
beside her some guy with a ski cap, both awake, and
simultaneously a brunette girl looking like some artist

gal beatnik gal in Greenwich Village comes in—Then
I see ten, maybe eight other people all milling around
in the corners with spoons and matches—One of them
is a typical junkey, that rugged tenderness, those rough
and suffering features covered with a gray sick slick, the
eyes certainly alert, the mouth alert, hat, suit, watch,
spoon, heroin, working swiftly at shots—Everybody is
shooting up—Tristessa is called by one of the men and
she rolls up her coat sleeve—Cruz too—The ski cap has
jumped out of bed and is doing the same—The Greenwich Village gal has somehow slipt into the bed, at the
foot, got her big sensuous body under the sheets from
the other end, and lies there, glad, on a pillow, watching—People come in and out from the village outdoors—
I expect to get a shot too and I say to one of the cats
"Poquito gote" which I imagine means little taste but
really means "little leak"—Leak indeed, I get nothing,
all my money's gone—

  The activity is furious, interesting, human, I watch
truly amazed, stoned as I am I can see this must be the
biggest junk den in Latin America—What interesting
types!—Tristessa is talking a mile a minute—The be-
hatted junkey with rough and tender features, with little
sandy mustache and faintly blue eyes and high cheekbones, is a Mexican but looks just like any junkey in New
York—He wont give me a shot either—I just sit and
wait—At my feet I have a half full bottle of beer Tristessa
had bought me en route, which I'd cached in clothes,
now I sip it in front of all these junkies and that finishes

my chances—I keep a sharp eye on the bed expecting
the fat lady to get up and leave, and the artist gal at her
feet, but only the men hustle and dress and get out and
finally we leave too—

"Where we goin?"

We walk outa there through a saddler's prompt line
of crossed sword eyes of miux ow you know, the old
gantlet line, of respectable bourgeois Mexicans in the
morning, but nobody stops us, no cops, we stumble out
and down a narrow dirt street and up to another door
and inside a little old court where an old man is sweeping
with a broom and inside you hear many voices—

He pleads with me with his eyes about something, like,
"Dont start trouble," I make the sign "*Me* start trouble?"
but he insists so I hesitate to go in but Tristessa and Cruz
drag me confidently and I look back at the old man who
has given his consent but is still pleading with his eyes—
Great God, he knew!

The place is a kind of unofficial morning snort-bar,
Cruz goes into dark noisy interiors and comes out with
a kind of weak anisette in a waterglass and I taste—I
dont want any particularly—I just stand against the dobe
wall looking at the yellow light—Cruz looks absolutely
crazy now, with high hairy bestial nostrils like in Orozco
the women screaming in revolutions but nevertheless
she manages to look dainty too—Besides she is a dainty
little person, I mean her heart, all night long she has
been very nice to me and she likes me—In fact she'd
screamed in a drunk one time "Tristessa you're jealous

because Yack wanted to marry me!"—and but she knows
I love unlovable Tristessa—so she's sistered me and I
liked it—some people have vibrations that come straight
from the vibrating heart of the sun, unjaded . . .

But as we're standing there Tristessa suddenly says:
"Yack" (me) "all night"—and she starts imitating my
shiver in the all-night street, at first I laugh, sun's yellow
hot now on my coat, but I feel alarmed to see her imitate
my shiver with such convulsive earnestness and Cruz
notices too and says "Stop Tristessa!" but she goes on,
her eyes wild and white, shivering her thin body in the
coat, her legs begin to crumple—I reach out laughing
"Ah come on"—she gets more shivery and convulsive
and suddenly (as I'm thinking "How can she love me
making fun of me *seriously* like that") she starts to fall,
which imitation is going too far, I try to grab her, she
bends way down to the ground and hangs a minute (just
like descriptions Bull had just given me of heroin addicts
nodding down to their shoetops on Fifth Avenue in the
20's Era, way down till their head hung completely from
the necks and there was nowhere to go but up or flat
down on the head) and to my pain and crash Tristessa
just bonks her skull and falls headlong on it right on the
harsh stone and collapses.

"Oh no Tristessa!" I cry and grab her under the arms
and twist her over and sit her in my haunches as I hunch
against the wall—She is breathing heavily and suddenly
I see blood all over her coat—

"She's dying," I think, "suddenly she's decided now

to die . . . This insane morning, this insane minute"—
And here's the old man with the pleading eyes still looking at me with his broom and men and women going
in for anisette stepping right over us (with gingerly unconcern but slowly, scarcely glancing down)—I put my
head to hers, cheek to cheek, and hold her tight, and
say "*Non non non non*" and what I mean is "Dont die"—
Cruz is on the ground with us on the other side, crying—
I hold Tristessa by her little ribs and pray—Blood now
trickles out of her nose and mouth—

No one's gonna move us outa that doorway—this I
swear—

I realize I'm there to refuse to let her die—

We get water, on my big red bandana, and mop her
a little—After whiles of convulsive shuddering suddenly
she becomes extremely calm and opens her eyes and
even looks up—She wont die—I feel it, she wont die,
not in my arms nor right now, but I feel too "She must
know that I refused and now she'll be expecting me to
show her something better than that—than death's eternal ecstasy"—O Golden Eternity, and as I know death
is best but "Non, I love you, dont die, dont leave me . . .
I love you too much"—"Because I love you isnt that
enough reason to try to live?"—O the gruesome destiny
of we human beings, each one of us will suddenly at
some terrible moment die and frighten all our lovers
and carrion the world—and crack the world—and all
the heroin addicts in all the yellow cities and sandy des-
erts cannot care—and they'll die too—

Tristessa now tries to get up, I raise her by little broken armpits, she leans, we adjust her coat, poor coat, we wipe off a little blood—Start off—Start off in the yellow Mexican morning, not dead—I let her walk by herself ahead of us, lead the Way, she does so through incredibly dirty staring streets full of dead dogs, past gawking children and old women and old men in dirty rags, out to a field of rocks, across that we stumble—Slowly—I can sense it now in her silence, "*This* is what you give me instead of death?"—I try to know what to give her instead—No such thing better than death—All I can do is stumble behind her, sometimes I briefly lead the way but I'm not much the figure of the man, The Man Who Leads The Way—But I know she is dying now, either from epilepsy or heart, shock, or goofball convulsion, and because of that no landlady is going to stop me from taking her home to my room on the roof and letting her sleep and rest under my open sleepbag, with Cruz and me both,— I tell her that, we get a cab and start to Bull's—We get off there, they wait in the cab as I knock on his window for the money for the cab—

"*You cant bring Cruz here!*" he yells. "Neither one of em!" He hands me the money, I pay the cab, the girls get out, and there's Bull's big sleepy face in the door saying "No No—the kitchen is full of women, they'll never let you through!"

"But she's dying! I've got to take care of her!"

I turn and I see both their coats, the back of their coats, have majestically Mexicanly womanly turned, with

immense dignity, streaks of dust and all street plaster
and all, together, the two ladies go down the sidewalk
slowly, the way Mexican women aye French Canadian
women go to church in the morning—There is something unalterable in the way both their coats have turned
on the women in the kitchen, on Bull's worried face, on
me—I run after them—Tristessa looks at me seriously'
"I go down to Indio for to get a shot" and in that way
that normal way she always says that, as if (I guess, I'm
a liar, watch out!) as if she means it and really wants to
go get that shot—

And I had said to her "I wanta sleep where you sleep
tonight" but fat chance of me getting into Indio's or even
herself, his wife hates her—They walk majestically, I
hesitate majestically, with majestic cowardice, fearing the
women in the kitchen who have barred Tristessa from
the house (for breaking everything in her goofball fits)
and barred her above all from passing through that
kitchen (the only way to my room) up narrow ivorytower
winding iron steps that shiver and shake—

"They'd never let you through!" yells Bull from the
door. "Let em go!"

One of the landladies is on the sidewalk, I'm too
ashamed and drunk to look her in the eye—

"But I'll tell them she's dying!"

"Come in here! Come in here!" yells Bull. I turn,
they've got their bus at the corner, she's gone—

Either she'll die in my arms or I'll hear about it—

What shroud was the reason why darkness and heaven

commingled to come and lay the mantle of sorrow on the hearts of Bull, El Indio and me, who all three love her and weep in our thoughts and know she will die— Three men, from three different nations, in the yellow morning of black shawls, what was the angelic demonic power that devised this?—What's going to happen?

At night little Mexican cop whistles blow that all is well, and all is all wrong, all is tragic,—I dont know what to say.

I'm only waiting to see her again—

And only last year she'd stood in my room and said "A friend is better than pesos, a friend that geev it to you in the bed" when still she believed anyway we'd get our tortured bellies together and get rid of some of the pain—Now too late, too late—

In my room at night, the door open, I watch to see her come in, as if she could get through that kitchen of women—And for me to go looking for her in Mexico Thieves' Market, that's I suppose what I'll have to do—

Liar! Liar! I'm a liar!

And supposing I go find her and she wants to hit me over the head again, I know it's not her it's the goof-balls—but where could I take her, and what would it solve to sleep with her?—a softest kiss from pale-rosest lips I did get, in the street, another one of those and I'm gone—

My poems stolen, my money stolen, my Tristessa dying, Mexican buses trying to run me down, grit in the sky, agh, I never dreamed it could be this bad—

And she hates me—Why does she hate me?
Because I'm so smart

"AS SURE AS you're sittin there," Bull keeps saying
since that morning, "Tristessa'll be back tapping on that
window on the thirteenth for money for her con-
nection"—

He wants her to come back—

El Indio comes over, in black hat, sad, manly, Mayan
stern, preoccupied, "Where is Tristessa?" I ask, he says,
hands out, "I dont know."

Her blood is on my pants like my conscience—

But she comes back sooner than we expect, on the
night of the 9th—Right while we're sitting there talking
about her—She taps on the window but not only that
reaches in a crazy brown hand through the old hole
(where El Indio's a month ago put his fist through in a
rage over junkless), she grabs the great rosy curtains that
Bull junkey-wise hangs from ceiling to sill, she shivers
and shakes them and sweeps them aside and looks in
and as if to see we're not sneaking morphine shots on
her—The first thing she sees is my smiling turned face—
It must of disgusted the hell out of her—"Bool—Bool—"

Bool hastily dresses to go out and talk to her in the
bar across the street, she's not allowed in the house.

"Aw let her in"

"*I cant*"

We both go out, I first while he locks, and there confronted by my "great love" on the sidewalk in the dim evening lights all I can do is shuffle awhile and wait in the line of time—"How you?" I do say—

"Okay"

Her left side of face is one big dirty bandage with black caked blood, she has it hidden under her head-shawl, holds it draped there—

"Where that happen, with me?"

"No, after I leave you, *tree times* I fall"—She holds up three fingers—She's had three further convulsions—The cotton batting hangs down and there are long strip tails down to almost her chin—She would look awful if she wasnt holy Tristessa—

Bull comes out and slowly we go across the street to the bar, I run to her other side to gentleman her, O what an old sister I am—It's like Hong Kong, the poorest sampan maids and mothers of the river in Chinee slacks propelling with the Venetian steer-pole and no rice in the bowl, even they, in fact they especially have their pride and would put down an old sister like me and O their beautiful little cans in sleek shiney silk, O—their sad faces, high cheekbones, brown color, eyes, they look at me in the night, at all Johns in the night, it's their last resort—O I wish I could write!—Only a beautiful poem could do it!

How frail, beat, final, is Tristessa as we load her into the quiet hostile bar where Madame X sits counting her pesos in the back room, facing all, and lil mustachio'd

anxious bartender darts furtively to serve us, and I offer
Tristessa a chair that will hide her sad mutilated face
from Madame X but she refuses and sits any old way—
What a threesome in a bar usually reserved for Army
officers and Mex businessmen foaming their mustaches
at mugs of afternoon!—Tall bony frightening hump-
backed Bull (what do the Mexicans think of him?) with
his owlish glasses and his slow shaky but firm-going walk
and me the baggy-trousered gringo jerk with combed
hair and blood and paint on his jeans, and she, Tristessa,
wrapt in a purple shawl, skinny,—poor,—like a vendor
of loteria tickets in the street, like doom in Mexico—I
order a glass of beer to make it look good, Bull con-
descends to coffee, the waiter is nervous—

O headache, but there she is sitting next to me, I drink
her in—Occasionally she turns those purple eyes at me—
She is sick and wants a shot, Bull no got—But she will
now go get three gramos on the black market—I show
her the pictures I've been painting, of Bull in his chair
in purple celestial opium pajamas, of me and my first
wife ("Mi primera esposa," she makes no comment, her
eyes look briefly at each picture)—Finally when I show
her my painting "candle burning at night" she doesnt
even look—They're talking about junk—All the time I
feel like taking her in my arms and squeezing her,
squeezing that little frail unobtainable not-there body—

The shawls falls a little and her bandage shows in the
bar—miserable—I dont know what to do—I begin to get
mad—

Finally she's talking about her friend's husband who's put her out of the house that day by calling the cops (he a cop himself), "He call cops because I no give im my *body*" she says nastily—

Ah, so she thinks of her body as some prize she shant give away, to hell with her—I pivot in my feelings and brood—I look at her feelingless eyes—

Meanwhile Bull is warning her about goofballs and I remind her that her old ex-lover (now dead junkey) had told me too never to touch them—Suddenly I look at the wall and there are the pictures of the beautiful broads of the calendar (that Al Damlette had in his room in Frisco, one for each month, over tokay wine we used to revere them), I bring Tristessa's attention to them, she looks away, the bartender notices, I feel like a beast—

AND ALL THE previous ensalchichas and papas fritas of the year before, Ah Above, what you doin with your children?—You with your sad compassionate and nay-would-I-ever-say unbeautiful face, what you doin with your stolen children you stole from your mind to think a thought because you were bored or you were Mind— shouldna done it, Lord, Awakenerhood, shouldna played the suffering-and-dying game with the children in your own mind, shouldna slept, shoulda whistled for the music and danced, alone, on a cloud, yelling to the stars you made, God, but never shoulda thought up and topped up tippy top Toonerville tweaky little sorrowers like us, the children—Poor crying Bull—child, when's sick, and I cry too, and Tristessa who wont even let herself cry . . .

OH WHAT WAS the racket that backeted and smashed in raging might, to make this oil-puddle world?—

Because Tristessa needs my help but wont take it and I wont give—yet, supposing everybody in the world devoted himself to helping others all day long, because of a dream or a vision of the freedom of eternity, then wouldnt the world be a garden? A Garden of Arden, full of lovers and louts in clouds, young drinkers dreaming and boasting on clouds, gods—Still the god's'd'a fought? Devote themselves to gods-dont-fight and bang! Miss Goofball would ope her rosy lips and kiss in the World all day, and men would sleep—And there wouldnt be men or women, but just one sex, the original sex of the mind—But that day's so close I could snap my finger and it would show, what does *it* care? . . . About this recent little event called the world.

"I love Tristessa," nevertheless I have the gall to stay and say, to both of them—"I woulda told the landladies I love Tristessa—I can tell them she's sick—She needs help—She can come sleep in my room tonight"—

Bull is alarmed, his mouth opens—O the old cage, he

loves her!—You should see her puttering around the
room cleaning up while he sits and cuts up his junk with
a razorblade, or just sits saying "M-m-m-m-m-m-m-m"
in long low groans that arent groans but his message
and song, now I begin to realize Tristessa wants Bull to
be her husband—

"I wanted Tristessa to be my third wife," I say later—
"I didnt come to Mexico to be told what to do by old
sisters? Right in front of the faculty, shooting?—Listen
Bull and Tristessa, if Tristessa dont care then I dont
care—" At this she looks at me, with surprised not-sur-
prised round she-doesnt-care-eyes—"Give me a shot of
morphine so I can think the way you do."

They promptly give me that, in the room later on,
meanwhile I've been drinking mescal again—" All or
nothing at all," says I to Bull, who repeats it—

"I'm not a whore," I add—And I also want to say
"Tristessa is not a whore" but I dont want to bring up
the subject—Meanwhile she changes completely with her
shot, feels better, combs her hair to a beautiful black
sheen, washes her blood, washes her whole face and
hands in a soapy washtub like Long Jim Beaver up on
the Cascades by his campfire—Swoosh—And she rubs
the soap thoroughly in her ears and twists fingertips in
there and makes squishy sounds, wow, washing, Charley
didnt have a beard last night—She cowls her head again
with the now-brushed shawl and turns to present us, in
the lightbulbed high-ceiling room, a charming Spanish
beauty with a little scar on her brow—The color of her

face is really tan (she calls herself dark, "As Negra as
me?") but in the lights that shine her face keeps changing,
sometimes it is jet-brown almost black-blue (beautiful)
with outlines of sheeny cheek and long sad mouth and
the bump on her nose which is like Indian women in
the morning in Nogales on a high dry hill, the women
of the various guitar—The Castilian touch, though it
may be only as Castilian as old Zacatecas it is fitting—
She turns, neat, and I notice she *has* no body at all, it
is utterly lost in a little skimpy dress, then I realize she
never eats, "her body" (I think) "must be beautiful"—
"beautiful little thing"—

But then Bull explains: "She dont want love—You put
Grace Kelly in this chair, Muckymuck's morphine on
that chair, Jack, I take the morphine, I no take the Grace
Kelly."

"Yes," asserts Tristessa, "and me, I no awanta love."

I dont say nothin about love, like I dont start singing
"Love is a completely endless thing, it's the April row
when feelers reach for everything" and I dont sing
"Embraceable You" like Frank Sinatra nor that "Tow-
ering Feeling" Vic Damone says "the touch of your hand
upon my brow, the look in your eyes I see," wow, no,
I dont disagree or agree with this pair of love-thieves,
let em get married and get under—go under the sheets—
go bateau'ing in Roma—Gallo—anywhere—me, I'm not
going to marry Tristessa, Bull is—She putters around
him endlessly, how strangely while I'm lying on the bed
junk-high she comes over and cleans up the headboard

with her thighs practically in my face and I study them
and old Bull is watching out of the top of his glasses to
the side—Min n Bill n Mamie n Ike n Maroney Maroney
Izzy and Bizzy and Dizzy and Bessy Fall-me-my-closer
Martarky and Bee, O god their names, their names, I
want their names, Amie n Bill, not Amos n Andy, open
the mayor (my father did love them) open the crocus
the mokus in the closet (this Freudian sloop of the mind)
(O slip slop) (slap) this old guy that's always—Molly!—
Fibber M'Gee be jesus and Molly—Bull and Tristessa,
sitting there in the house all night, moaning over their
razor-blades and white junk and pieces of broken mirror
to act as the pan (the diamond sharp junk that cuts into
glass)—Quiet evenings at home—Clark Gable and Mona
Lisa—

Yet—"Hey, Tristessa I live with you and Bull pay" I
say finally—

"I dont care," she says, turning to me on the stool—
"It's awright with me."

"Wont you at least pay half of her rent?" asks Bull,
noting in his notebook figures he keeps all the time.
"Will you say yes or no."

"You can go see her when you want," he adds.

"No, I wanted to live with her."

"Well, you cant do that—you havent got the money."

But Tristessa keeps looking at me and I keep staring
at her, suddenly we love each other as Bull drones on
and I admire her openly and she shines openly—Earlier,
I'd grabbed her, when she said "You remember every-

thing the other night?"—"Yes"—"in the street, how you
kiss me"—And I show her how she'd kissed me.

That little gentle brush of the lips on the lips, with
just the slightest kiss, to indicate kiss—She'd shined on
that one—She didnt care—

She had no money to take the cab home, no bus was
running, we had no more money any of us (except
money in the bloodbank) (money in the mudbank, Charley)—"Yes, I walk home."

"Three miles, two miles," I say, and there was that
long walk through the rain I remembered—"You can
come up there," pointing to my room on the roof, "I
wont bother you, no te molesta."

"No te molesta" but I would leave her molest me—
Old Bull is glancing over his glasses and paper, I've
screwed everything up with the mama again, Oedipus
Rex, I'll tear out my eyes in the morning—San Francisco,
New York, Padici, Medu, Mantua or anywhere, I'm always the King sucker who was made out to be the po-
sitional son in woman and man relationships, Ahh-
yaaaaa—(Indian howl in the night, to campo-country
sweet musica)—"King, bing, I'm always in the way for
momma and poppa—When am I gonna be poppa?"

"NO TE MOLESTA," and too, for Bull, my poppa,—I
said: "I'd have to be a junkey to live with Tristessa, and
I cant be a junkey."

"Aint nobody knows junkies like another junkey."

I gulp to hear the truth, too—

"Besides, too, Tristessa is an oldtime junkey, like me, she no chicken—in junk—Junkies are very strange persons."

Then he would launch into a long story about the strange persons he's known, in Riker's Island, in Lexington, in New York, in Panama—in Mexico City, in Annapolis—In keeping with his strange history, which included opium dreams of strange tiered racks where girls are being fed opium through dreamy blue tubes, and similar strange episodes like all the innocent *faux pas* he'd made, tho always with an evil greed just before it, he'd thrown up at Annapolis after a binge, in the showers, and to conceal it from his officers he'd tried to wash it down with the hot water, with the result the smell permeated "all of Bradley Hall" and there was a beautiful poem written about it in the newspaper of the Navy Goats—He would launch into long stories but she was there and with her he just conducted routine junkey talk in baby Spanish, like, "You no go tomorrow good look like that."

"Yes, I clean my face now."

"It no look good—They take one look at you and they know you takin too many secanols"

"Yes, I go"

"I brush your coat—" Bull gets up and helps clean her things—

To me he says, "Them artists and writers, they dont

like to work—Dont believe in work" (as the year before,
as Tristessa and Cruz and I chatted gayly with the gaiety
I had last year, in the room, he's banging with a Mayan
stone statue about the size of a big fist trying to fix the
door he'd broken down the night before because he took
too many goofballs and went out of his room and
locked-clicked the padlock, key in the room and him in
his pajamas at One A M)—wow, I do gossippy—(So he'd
yelled at me "Come help me fix this door, I cant do this
by myself"—"Oh yes you can, I'm talking"—"You artists
are all lazy bums")

Now to prove I'm not like that I get up slowly, dizzy
from that shot of their love stuff, and get some water
in the tin pitcher to heat on the upturned ray-lamp so's
Tristessa can have hot water for her wound-wash—but
I hand him the pitcher because I cant go thru the hassel
of balancing it on the flimsy wires and anyway he's the
old master Old Wizard Old Water Witch Doctor who
can do it and wont let me try it—Then I get back on the
bed, prostrate—prostate gland too, as morphine takes
all the sex out of your parts and leaves it somewhere
else, in your gut—Some people are all guts and no
heart—I take heart—You shoot spades—You drink
clubs—You blast oranges—I take heart and bat—Two—
Three—Ten trillion million dizzying powder of stars
fermangitatin in the high blue Jack Shaft—prop—I dont
drown no buddies in oil—I got no guts to do it—Got
heart not to—But the sex, when the morphine is loosed
in your flesh, and slowly spreads, hot, and headies your

brain, the sex recedes into the gut, most junkies are thin, Bull and Tristessa are both bags of bones—

But O the grace of some bones, that milt a little flesh hang-on, like Tristessa, and makes a woman—And Old Bull, spite of his thin hawky body nobody, his gray hair is well slicked and his cheek is youthful and sometimes he looks positively pretty, and in fact Tristessa had finally one night decided to make it and he was there and they made it, good—I wanted some of that too, seein's how Bull didnt rise to the issue except once every twenty years or so—

But no, that's enough, hear no more, Min n Molly n Bill n Gregory Pegory Fibber McGoy, oy, I'd leave them be and go my own way—"Find me a Mimi in Paris, a Nicole, a sweet Tathagata Pure Pretty Piti"—Like poems spoke by old Italians in South American palm mud, flat, who wanta go back to Palabbrio, reggi, and stroll the beauteous bell-ringing girl-walking boulevard and drink aperitif with the coffee muggers of the card street—O movie—A movie by God, showing us him—him,—and us showing him,—him which is us—for how can there be two, not-one? Palmsunday me that, Bishop San Jose . . .

I'll go light candles to the Madonna, I'll paint the Madonna, and eat ice cream, benny and bread—"Dope and saltpork," as Bhikku Booboo said—I'll go to the South of Sicily in the winter, and paint memories of Arles—I'll buy a piano and Mozart me that—I'll write long sad tales about people in the legend of my life— This part is my part of the movie, let's hear yours